jill marshall recently moved from the United Kingdom to New Zealand, along with her small daughter and her even smaller mad dog. Her childhood ambition was to become an author, so in 2001 Jill gave up her career at a huge international company to concentrate on writing for children. When not working, writing and being a mum, Jill plays guitar, takes singing lessons and is learning to play the drum kit she has set up in the garage. One day she might even sing in a band again . . .

Look out for the third book in the
jane blonde series:

jane blonde, twice the spylet.

Jane Blonde

spies trouble

JILL MARSHALL

MACMILLAN CHILDREN'S BOOKS

First published 2006 by Macmillan Children's Books
a division of Macmillan Publishers Limited
20 New Wharf Road, London N1 9RR
Basingstoke and Oxford
www.panmacmillan.com

Associated companies throughout the world

ISBN-13: 978-0-330-43825-4
ISBN-10: 0-330-43825-5

1 3 5 7 9 8 6 4 2

A CIP catalogue record for this book is available from
the British Library.

Typeset by Nigel Hazle
Printed and bound in Great Britain by Mackays of Chatham plc, Kent

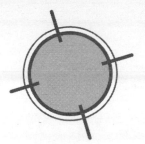

groovelicious gratitude to rachel and the whole
of the macmillan bunch for being a writer's
dream team, to glenys for ceiling-scraping
and black-hole digging, to friends and family on
this side of the world and the other for putting
up with me and putting me up, and to all those
spylets-in-training who read 'jane blonde,
sensational spylet'. you rock!

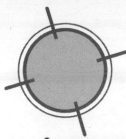

**for mum and dad, who aren't superspies –
just super people**

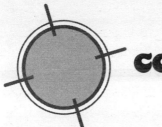

contents

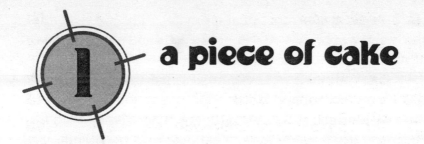

a piece of cake

The cubicle fizzed as Jane Blonde, Sensational Spylet, stepped into the Wower to be changed back into an almost normal schoolgirl once more.

It had become such a familiar routine that she barely noticed the pearlescent moisture drops swirling around her inside the glittering spy-shower cubicle. Blonde was already thinking about what she had to do when she got out of the Wower. Her SPI:KE (Solomon's Polificational Investigations: Kid Educator) was in the Spylab, chewing anxiously on a carrot stick as she awaited a debrief from her prize pupil. In fact, her only pupil.

There wasn't long to wait. Within a few moments a robotic hand had removed Jane Blonde's voice-activated Ultra-gog spy spectacles, so that her eyes dimmed a little to their usual misty grey. Her silver Lycra SPIsuit was removed, and the angular limbs beneath it were encased once again in regular school-holidays uniform: jeans and a 'Give Me Sunshine' T-shirt. Finally, another metallic hand whisked the bright platinum colour from her hair, along with the band that had held it firmly in place in a high, multi-functional ponytail. The Spylet's fine mousey waves settled on to her shoulders, and Janey Brown emerged from the Wower.

Janey grinned as G-Mamma rifled through her large stainless-steel fridge. 'Is this what you're looking for?'

G-Mamma seized the tatty box before Janey even had her arm fully extended. 'That was mean, Blonde-girl. Mean, mean, mean. You know the order you're meant to do this in: decode, debrief, de-Wow. Since when did you start de-Wowing before you gave me the goodies? I mean, the crucial info.'

'Just trying to help you stick to your diet, G-Mamma. You said that was my mission for the holidays,' Janey said teasingly.

G-Mamma rolled her Amethyst-Dazzled eyes heavenwards. 'That was just a trick, Blondette! I was bluffing! You were meant to see straight through it immediately and do the reverse: BRING ME CAKE!'

'Well, I worked it out in the end,' said Janey. 'Unfortunately the only place to get cake at midnight was from the bins behind the bakeries. I chose the cleanest bin I could find. The cake's probably only a day or two old . . .'

'It's been through the Wower though!' G-Mamma's eyes gleamed as she pulled a very smart cake box complete with ribbon out of the cubicle. 'Look at that baby.'

Janey laughed. The rather squashed and miserable Victoria sponge she had raised from the depths of the dustbin had been upgraded to a mighty gateau. Light-as-air angel cake interspersed with hefty layers of jam, cream and butter icing made its way into the cavern of G-Mamma's mouth. 'Save me some!' said Janey. 'That looks amazing. I didn't know the Wower worked on food as well as people. Oh, and cats.'

She looked around the lab for her Spycat, Trouble. Since being embroiled in Janey's first mission, Trouble had become very attached to her and now spent most of his time on the other side of G-Mamma's fireplace, in Janey's bedroom, although the smell of cream cakes and doughnuts often enticed him back to G-Mamma's lab. 'Where is he then? Have you seen him tonight?'

G-Mamma shook her head. 'He's a cat, girly-girl. He's probably out chasing mice.'

'He hates mice.'

'True. Well, chasing birdies then.'

'It's night-time.'

G-Mamma tutted. 'The kitty's fine. Now listen, it's the end of the holidays, and I want to show Solomon how much we've done since you saw him last.' She reached out for a ruler, dropped a little kiss on to it and pointed one end at Janey. A tiny pinprick of green light danced before her. 'Speak. Tell your father what you've learned in the last couple of weeks.'

The ruler was actually a LipSPICK (Lip-activated SPI-Camera Kilobank) – a spy camera with an enormous memory. Janey stared into the winking light and took a deep breath. When she went back to school tomorrow she would have to write a report about what she'd done

3

in the holidays. There was no way she would be able to say what had really happened that summer: that a mad woman called G-Mamma had turned up to inform her that Janey was actually a spy (well, a Spylet), spy-name Jane Blonde; that her never-seen-before Uncle Solomon was actually the head of the mighty Solomon's Polifications Investigations (SPI) and had disappeared with a secret so huge that it could change the world, since it allowed for one creature to be frozen and changed into another, completely different animal; that her lovely teacher and nice new friend Freddie were actually leading members of the evil rogue spy organization Sinerlesse, which Janey had had to thwart on her first mission. She certainly couldn't write that the head teacher and her son, Alfie, were really a SPI and Spylet, and her greatest friends and supporters.

And there was an even greater revelation. Her Uncle Solomon was really her father, Boz Brilliance Brown, who Janey had thought had died before her birth and whom her (now very ordinary) mother, Jean Brown, had partnered in her previous life as the superSPI Gina Bellarina. It was all so crazy that Janey could hardly believe it herself.

'Come on,' muttered G-Mamma indistinctly through a fifth mouthful of gateau. 'Spill the beanage.'

'OK.' Janey ticked off the various things she had learned over the last couple of weeks in her spy lessons. 'Body language: I've learned how to make myself blend into a crowd without being seen, or how to stand out so all attention is on me if I'm the decoy. And I can read other people's body language to know if they're lying. Codes: I've covered half a dozen different encryptions. I've learned that a single hair can tell you if someone's been looking at your stuff, and I can take fingerprints with talcum powder. Equipment: I've mastered the Girl-gauntlet and my Fleet-feet technique. My self-defence is getting much better but I know the best way for me to stay unhurt is to get out of the way. Um, I guess that's the lot.' Janey smiled into the camera a little shyly.

'Excellent briefing, Blonde.' G-Mamma held the ruler out to Janey. 'Now you hold it and turn it on me. I've prepared something a little special for Solomon.'

As Janey directed the camera G-Mamma whipped a lime-green cloth off the nearby counter and flicked a switch on the twin speakers that were hidden beneath it. A pounding rhythm filled the Spylab, and Janey's SPI:KE popped her head in time, from one side to the other.

Janey screwed up her eyes. 'Oh no, I think I know what's coming.'

'Yo, Sol!' yelled G-Mamma, flinging her hips around with wild abandon. 'Here we go . . .

> *'Your girl's been SPI:KED, and I hope you liked*
> *What she had to say on graduation day.*
> *A Spylet true is what I have for you*
> *And a badge of honour is what you're gonna gonna gonna*
> *   gonna . . .*
> *GIVE BLONDE!'*

5

Janey smiled hesitantly. G-Mamma had so much enthusiasm that it was difficult to avoid admiring her for it. 'So I've graduated? Wow. How are you going to get this message to Solomon?'

'You're all Spylet now, honey. Yes, you are. And a Spylet should be able to work out the answer to that second question.' G-Mamma turned off the beat box to allow Janey some peace to think.

'Well, we don't know where he is,' said Janey, 'so we can't send it by post. Right. He's not going to drop round here to collect it either, so . . . ah . . . got it! He can collect the image from anywhere, wherever he is, provided he has the right password, or . . . or no, the right lip-print activation?'

G-Mamma's round blue eyes shimmered. 'Oh, girl, I trained you well. How spiky is that SPI:KEd spylet? Very very, yes indeedy. Correct answer. Full points.'

'So can I have some cake now?'

'No way. Too late. You'll get indigestion. And it's school in the morning. So through the tunnel and into bed with you.'

G-Mamma shoved her towards the fireplace as Janey protested. 'You're starting to sound like my mum.'

Dropping to her knees, Janey shimmied through the short tunnel that ran between their two fireplaces and brushed herself down on her bedroom hearth before carrying out what was now her usual, secret night-time routine.

Swallowing down the guilty feeling that hit her in the

gullet each time she did this, Janey pulled out the old shoebox containing her precious collection of SPI-buys – gadgets her father had sent her over the years. It had once contained perfume that was really SPIT (SPI-Truth serum), a spy pen with invisible ink, rocket-powered hairslides and a LipSPICK ruler of her own. Now all that remained were a few drops of SPIT and a miniscule disc of metal from the LipSPICK. It was this tiny circle that she now balanced on the end of her finger like someone about to put in a contact lens. Instead of pushing it in her eye, however, she drew it to her mouth and, very gently, gave it a feathery kiss.

'Hello,' she whispered, as a moving image sprang up above her head.

The flickering light in Janey's bedroom caught the eye of the spy lurking outside in the garden. He turned his head slowly to the window, as if it was weighed down by the strange mask he wore – a circle made up of large jagged spikes. His Ultra-gogs were built into the narrow eye-slits cut into the metal.

'X-ray,' he instructed under his breath, 'and zoom.'

There it was again, on the ceiling – footage of a man stroking the head of a large tabby kitten and mouthing something to the camera. The spy caught his breath and focused the Ultra-gogs to lip-read what the man was saying, over and over again.

'. . . what I've created . . . what I've created . . . what I've created . . .'

The spy smiled. From here on in, it was going to be plain sailing.

'Thank you, my dear,' he whispered. And then he was gone.

 steaming star signs

The next morning Janey jumped out of the Clean Jean minivan at the school gates. 'Have a good day!' shouted her mother, already reversing as she sped off to her early supermarket cleaning job.

'I will. Bye, Mum.' Janey grinned. It was a ridiculous-looking van, with an oversized dustpan and brush perched on the top like a cherry on a cake, and feather dusters for windscreen wipers. But at least now she always knew exactly when her mum (or one of the three other vans in Jean Brown's little cleaning empire) was approaching.

'Morning,' said a voice behind her. 'Great wheels. You must be so proud.'

It was Alfie Halliday, Class Superstar, also known as Al Halo, Spylet, and now one of Janey's best friends. Janey whacked him on the arm with her bag. 'Actually I am. My mum's clever, and brave. She set up Clean Jean all by herself.'

'That's right. She's like Wonder Woman in an overall,' drawled Alfie. Luckily, Janey was fully aware that really he liked her mum and knew that she had once been Gina Bellarina, superSPI, until she'd been brain-wiped to keep her safe.

They made their way to their classroom and Janey plonked herself down at her desk, behind Alfie's. She held back a yawn.

'Hey, I graduated last night. It was a bit of a late one. I hope this new Mr Saunders is interesting enough to keep me awake this morning,' she whispered to Alfie.

'Just be glad he's not trying to kill you,' he hissed back. Their last teacher, the evil Miss Rale, was now seeing out her days as a mink, having been transformed by Janey's dad.

They soon discovered that Mr Saunders was a completely different kettle of fish – he was totally, utterly dull. As Janey had predicted, the new teacher began by asking the class to write an essay on 'What I did in the holidays'. Janey was careful to leave out any mention of the exciting spy-life she had been leading at night, and she lied a great deal about cleaning and trips to the swimming pool.

As the morning progressed there was only one matter of even vague interest. At ten o'clock Mr Saunders checked his watch and shot outside for a moment. He held open the door as he came back, and in shuffled a scared-looking girl with deep brown hair and skin the colour of caramel. Janey's heart went out to her immediately.

'Class, this is Paulette Solay, who has just moved here from . . .' Mr Saunders looked down at the girl. 'Sorry, where was it again?'

'France,' said Paulette quietly.

'That's right. Now, Paulette is joining our class, so I'd

like you all to help her to settle in. She's been at an international school until now, so I expect this will all feel a bit
different for her. Paulette, go and take a seat next to . . .'

Pick me, pick me, thought Janey, holding her breath.

'. . . Alfie Halliday. He knows his way around the
place pretty well. Well, he should do, he's the headmistress's son. Alfie, look after Paulette, will you?'

'Sure,' said Alfie, pulling out the chair next to him.
Paulette sat down shyly.

Janey knew just how Paulette felt. Before she'd
learned that she was a Spylet, she'd been afraid of her own
shadow. And Alfie, so confident and capable, had made
her feel completely inferior. She resolved to make friends
with Paulette and ensure the new girl settled in.

'Right, finish off your essays and we'll make a start on
some real work.' Mr Saunders turned to the blackboard.
'Maths books open at page seventeen, please.'

Janey looked down at her long divisions. She was
quite good at maths – it was just more puzzles to solve, as
far as she was concerned. She just didn't feel like doing it
right now. The room was clammy from all the wet coats
drying on the backs of chairs, and she could feel her fine
hair frizzing up at the ends. Bored, she looked over at
the window.

And sat bolt upright.

Something had appeared on one of the steamed-
up window panes. Janey poked Alfie in the back and
nodded towards the window when he turned
around.

He frowned quickly, then stuck up his hand. 'Mr Saunders, do you mind if I let some air in?'

'I suppose it is a bit stuffy in here,' said the teacher. 'Go ahead.'

Alfie flitted across the classroom and opened the window. Janey was probably the only one who noticed him wiping the sleeve of his jumper across the damp glass before he returned to his desk. After twenty minutes of tortured waiting, while Janey wondered if it was just the doodling of some bored pupil or a death threat – a Spylet could never be too careful – Alfie slipped a scrap of paper on to her exercise book. Janey dropped it on to her lap and opened it carefully.

It was a large, scrappy-looking star, and in it were the words:

SCAT CAT!
RAT PACK!

Underneath Alfie had scrawled, 'Can't rub out, written from outside.'

Janey's eyes met Alfie's. He raised his eyebrows hopelessly and turned back to his work. Janey had no idea what the words meant either, but all her spy instincts were tingling with anticipation.

When the bell rang for mid-morning break Alfie turned around quickly. 'Let's go and ask Mum.'

They were just about to run out of the room when a small voice said, 'Please. What we do?'

Paulette looked sorrowfully from Alfie to Janey like a lost puppy. Janey made her mind up quickly. 'Alfie's going to take you to the tuck shop. I have to go and see the headmistress.'

Alfie winked and led Paulette down the corridor as Janey ran off in the other direction.

'Janey!' said Mrs Halliday as she opened the door to her office. 'Is everything all right?'

Janey closed the door carefully. 'I'm not sure. This was written on the window – on the outside. I've got a funny feeling about it.'

Mrs Halliday studied the note. 'Well, that is a bit peculiar. Do you think it was one of the pupils, just messing about? '

'Can't be. They'd need a ladder. It's too far from the ground.'

'Good point,' said Mrs Halliday. 'What on earth can it mean?'

There was something familiar nagging at Janey. Reaching beneath her jumper, she pulled out a necklace with a chunky pendant hanging from it.

'Janey! You know the rules – no jewellery in school!' said Mrs Halliday sternly.

'But it's my SPIV!' Surely Mrs Halliday, spy-name Halo, recognized a SPI Visualator when she saw one?

'I don't know what you're talking about. Is that the name for necklaces nowadays?'

'But . . .'

Suddenly Janey realized that another pupil was

peering round the office door. Mrs Halliday nodded smartly. 'All right, Julian. Just give me two seconds. Janey was just going. Keep me posted on progress, won't you? It sounds like a *very* interesting project.'

Janey's heart pounded as she scurried down the corridor looking for somewhere quiet. Passing a narrow door, she stopped, pulled at the handle and slipped into the new caretaker's cupboard. A tiny radio was playing to itself. Janey moved it, along with some fluorescent green rubber gloves, and overturned the bucket they'd been resting on. Only when she had sat down did she dare to pull out her SPI Visualator again and hold it close to her mouth. 'G-Mamma! Are you there?'

A beaming round face appeared in the stone dangling from the necklace chain. 'Betcha boodles I'm here! What's the skinny, Blonde?'

'I'm not sure. I've just picked up a weird message at school. Is everything all right there?'

'It's candy-dandy, Blondette. Although I did just stand in the cat's food. Disgusting gloop between my toes. And I'd just painted them. It's not a good look!'

Janey frowned. 'Why hasn't Trouble eaten it? Did you give him cake last night?'

'I didn't see him last night. I thought he was with you. Oh, he'll just have gone off on one of his little kitty walkabouts.'

'I'm not so sure. I wonder . . .'

Trouble had been sent to G-Mamma for safe keeping by Janey's dad when he had been forced into hiding. *Scat*

Cat, the message had said. Was that a warning, or a threat? Whichever it was, Janey had a sudden urge to find her Spycat – quickly.

'G-Mamma,' she said softly, 'start looking for Trouble. Now.'

kittynapped

'What is that lunatic doing now?' asked Jean as they got out of the car after the school day had ended. Next door, a large body in satin pyjama bottoms and a sequinned poncho was wriggling around on the grass.

'Don't know.' Janey shrugged. Jean Brown disliked G-Mamma rather intensely, even though she couldn't exactly recall why. 'Maybe she's weeding?'

'Hmmmph,' sniffed her mother with her key in the door. 'She's the only weed round here. Sprouting up larger than life just where you don't want her.'

But right at that minute Janey did want her. Once inside, she took the stairs at a run. 'Just getting changed, Mum!'

'Fine, sweetheart. I'll start tea.'

Janey tapped on the wall to the top right of her fireplace and hopped around impatiently as the back panel of the fire slid upwards. As soon as there was a big enough gap she squatted down and wriggled through the short tunnel ahead of her.

She emerged in G-Mamma's gleaming Spylab. Her

SPI:KE had run inside and was sorting through a pile of frog-suits. 'Blonde, thank the stars you're here! You'll need one of these. Which do you fancy, aqua or fuchsia?'

Janey shook her head, puzzled. 'What do I need one of those for? Isn't my SPIsuit waterproof?'

'You need extra protection where you're going,' said G-Mamma darkly. 'I did as you said and went to look for Trouble. Well, I'm sorry to say that cat has vamooshed! Evaporated into thin air. But I found this under the hedge.'

G-Mamma pointed at a tiny piece of gauzy yellow rubber, split almost in two by what was quite clearly a claw mark.

'I've just analysed the material,' said G-Mamma, pointing at the computer screen. 'It's polypropylene, the type used in diving suits. Someone's kittynapped our wickle Twoubble. And whoever it is must have come from somewhere underwater.'

Janey thought hard. 'There isn't any water near here. Where would they have come from? It's not like there's a stream in the street. Even when it's raining, the water just goes . . . No!'

'What?' G-Mamma looked as innocent as possible, her eyebrows peaking under her crown of curls. 'What do you mean, no?'

Janey shook her head. 'I am not going down the drain.'

'But that's the only possibility! I checked!' said G-Mamma. 'There's a manhole cover right outside, and drippy drip-drops leading all the way to it. And our poor little kitty . . .'

'OK, OK.' Janey knew there was no way out of it. She had a duty to try to find Trouble. 'I'll take the aqua frog-suit,' said Janey, 'and a very big helmet.'

A minute or two later, Janey emerged from the Wower encased in glowing aqua rubber with her slick ponytail shimmering blonde. 'Will my Ultra-gogs work in . . . down there?'

'Think so!' G-Mamma answered brightly. 'Provided you don't get anything too gungy on them. Anyway, we don't have a helmet so they'll have to do. Here, chew this if you need to.'

Janey took hold of the rubbery creepy-crawly G-Mamma was offering her. 'Euw. Isn't it going to be bad enough down there?'

'It's gum.'

'Oh.' That was good. With pieces from Alfie's endless supply of gum, Janey had discovered she was a master bubble-blower, although she still wasn't allowed it at home.

'It's also a SPIder,' said G-Mamma. 'SPI Direct Energy Replenishment. In case you need some oxygen.'

For if I'm drowning, thought Janey. Great. She slid the SPIder into a pocket on her frog-suit sleeve and turned grimly to G-Mamma. 'I can't be gone long. Mum's making tea.'

'Well, let's get started then!'

G-Mamma bounded across her front lawn in short spiky movements. 'I know we haven't covered this yet in training, but I've worked out the angle of vision from each house in the street. We can't be seen if we follow this route exactly. Behind the bush, and . . . run! To the garden gnome, squat, CRAWL! OK.' She half stood as they reached the gate. 'Now, the manhole is just there. Go for it, Blondette! And take this torch.'

The manhole cover had not been pulled across properly, and Janey could see the tiny droplets of water around it that G-Mamma had mentioned. She also spotted something else – a couple of amber hairs sticking to the top rung of the ladder that led down into the drain. 'Trouble!' she gasped.

Janey edged one foot down to the next rung, then another, then another, until she squelched on to the floor of the drain, ankle-deep in sludge. It wasn't as bad as she'd suspected – hopefully it was just rainwater that came along this particular pipe.

'Right, G-Mamma, I'm going in!'

A sparkly taloned thumb appeared above the manhole in answer to Janey's hiss. 'Meet you back here.'

'OK.'

She set off resolutely. After she had sloshed along for a few minutes Janey came to a junction in the pipe. The single cylinder she'd been moving along forked, with equal-sized tunnels running off to the left and the right. There was nothing to indicate which one Trouble might have been taken along.

'Left,' said Janey instinctively. Her voice bounced back loudly from the tunnel walls. 'Oops,' she added more quietly, as she clambered into the left-hand pipe and set off along its length.

Good – there was a sign! Along the wall was a series of long scratches. Claw marks. Trouble had been trying to get out, scrambling to be dropped to the floor. It wouldn't have worried him in the slightest if he'd landed in water. Unusually for a cat, he loved it. Also unusually for a cat, he hated mice. When her father had learned how to transform one creature into another, he had turned a frog into a mouse right under Trouble's nose and the cat had never quite recovered from the shock. Janey suspected, however, that the type of vermin who lived down here was much bigger than mice: 'Rats!' she thought. 'Yuck.'

The water around her ankles began to run more swiftly. It was also becoming a little deeper, and she was beginning to recognize a familiar odour.

'What is that? Gas? No. Something . . .'

The odour reminded her of holidays, the school holidays she'd just had . . . and playing in the sunshine, and . . . The smell intensified and as it did so Janey heard a huge squelching gurgle. 'It's chlorine!' she realized. Was a swimming pool emptying? No . . .

The gurgling suddenly multiplied into a roar. Janey took off back along the tunnel towards the junction she had left only a few minutes before. Behind her there was a thunderous noise of surging water. She ran on, stumbling as she glanced over her shoulder. The roar became deafening, and now she could see it – a torrent of chlorinated water rushing towards her. At last she spotted the junction ahead, but the water was upon her now. She screamed as the deluge lifted her off her feet and sent her hurtling down the tunnel. She bobbed like a cork towards the surface, then realized with horror that the water was going to fill up the tunnel completely. She would run out of air before she managed to reach the junction and make her way back to the manhole.

The SPIder! As water gushed up over her ears, sloshing against her nose, her Ultra-gogs, her forehead, Janey delved in the pocket on her arm and seized the creepy-crawly gum. She pushed it towards her lips, fighting the pressure of the water as it closed in over her head.

And there it was – a sweet rush of oxygen down her throat. Janey chewed again and again and felt a bubble form inside her mouth. Two of the SPIder's legs poked through her lips and snaked up to her nose, forming a pincer on each nostril that pinched her nose shut. The body of the SPIder spread into a thin layer across her teeth, so that she could open her lips and breathe through her mouth. The other six legs anchored themselves to the inside of her mouth and shot air down into her lungs.

Now that she could breathe, Janey relaxed a little. She peered through her Ultra-gogs, which had stayed fixed to her face as if they were moulded on. The junction was coming up, but the water was rushing on down the tunnel that led to the manhole. She tried to anchor her feet against the walls of the tunnel, but the slippery surface and the rushing water prevented her. Forcing her head around, Janey beamed her laser up the tunnel behind her. A large brown object was hurtling towards her, spinning wildly as if trapped in a whirlpool. Trouble!

Janey noticed something glinting up ahead; it was a metal ring, probably used by workmen to hang a light on. It was the only thing to hang on to.

She grabbed it, but the ring was really only big enough for two fingers. Janey gripped tight as the water dragged at her, but her fingers were starting to ache. Any moment now they'd be ripped away by the torrent. She needed something to loop through the ring, but she was in a skintight frog-suit with not a dangly bit in sight. There was only one thing that would do.

Janey hauled herself up through the water by the tiny amount of grip she still had left in her numb fingers. Then, backing her head towards the ring and breathing steadily through the SPIder, she threaded her ponytail through the iron loop and took hold of the end. It worked. She was hanging from the ceiling of the tunnel by her hair.

The only problem was that she was now hanging face forward and couldn't see Trouble coming up behind her. She had to hope that he would see her and grab hold of her. She tried to make herself into as big a target as possible, stretching out into a star shape and trying to brace herself against the greasy sides of the pipe. Her feet slithered, and it took every scrap of effort she could muster to keep still. Just as she was thinking she would have to let go, she felt a small furry body whack into her shoulders and sink its talons in like crampons.

'Trouble, owwww! Claws in, you furball!' Unfortunately all that came out of her mouth was a string of bubbles. Blimey, how long does it take for a swimming pool to empty? Janey thought desperately. Trouble was hanging on, but he wouldn't be able to breathe . . .

Janey flexed her muscles against the pain. If the water didn't disappear by the time she'd counted to five, she would have to let go. One, two, three, four . . .

Just then the water dropped away to Janey's shoulders, then to her elbows, and finally to her thighs. With no water to take her weight, Janey's scalp howled in agony. She let go of her ponytail and managed to stand firm in the tumbling water. As she inhaled the air, the SPIder shrunk back into a normal-sized wad of gum, and Trouble jumped into the water beside her, bedraggled but otherwise none the worse for his adventure.

'Where have you been, Trubs?' Janey tousled his wet head. 'We were worried about you.' The cat blinked balefully at her. He didn't look as though he'd been especially worried himself. Janey grinned. 'Come on.'

As they walked along the tunnel to the manhole Trouble gave Janey occasional little licks with his raspy tongue. 'Nearly there, kitty.'

Suddenly G-Mamma's upside-down face blocked the light coming in through the manhole cover. 'Did you find him?'

'There you go,' said Janey, as she passed the sopping-wet cat up the ladder. 'I think he's been in a swimming pool.'

'OK. I'll take care of him, Blonde, but I gotta tell you, you've got trouble of your own. Your mum's been calling you for five minutes. Any second now she'll be up the stairs and in your room.'

'I so don't need this!' puffed Janey, hauling herself out of the manhole and through G-Mamma's garden. 'No time to de-Wow. We'll talk later about what's going on!'

Back in the Spylab, Janey shot through the fireplace tunnel into her bedroom and was just doing up the belt of her dressing gown when her mum opened the door.

'Janey, I've been shouting and shouting. Your tea is on the table.' Her mother eyed Janey suspiciously. 'Why are you wet?'

'I . . . I needed a shower,' Janey stammered.

Her mother sniffed. 'In bleach?'

Janey quickly trotted out yet another lie to her mother. Being an undercover agent demanded certain skills, and making up stories on the spot was one of them. 'They gave us this stuff at school. For . . . for head lice.'

Jean paused, then nodded sympathetically. 'OK. Better save some for me too. It's nothing to be ashamed of, sweetheart. You can tell me anything, you know!'

If only I could, thought Janey, peeling herself out of the aqua frog-suit a moment later. How much easier everything would be. As it was, she was going to have to endure a completely normal night of homework, bad cooking and reading in bed before she could get on to what she really wanted to do . . .

. . . spy.

clean machines

'Quickly, Janey, get in. I've got an appointment to keep,' said Jean Brown. 'You'll have to eat that on the go.'

'Can't you drop me at school first?' said Jancy through a mouthful of toast. She was anxious to meet up with Alfie and tell him about last night.

Her mum shook her head, crunching the van into gear. 'Sorry, I'm due there at eight. Anyway, I want you to come with me – I'd like your opinion. I'm thinking of a new venture for the Clean Jean Company.'

'But I really need . . . Oh, OK.'

Janey stopped short. There was no point going on. Her mum had a plan and she was going to stick to it, whatever Janey said. She sat in silence as they drove to the other side of town.

'Here we are,' said Jean, pulling the van through a set of huge metal gates. 'What do you think?'

They were in an oval yard like a racing track, with a narrow road leading around the edge and off to a large shed-like structure. Across the side of the building was a flourish of bold bronze writing, declaring: 'Rownigan's Car Wash. Make your car a star!'

'Great!' said Janey as a dusty white car, piebald with rust, nosed through the plastic doors to the shed. 'Car washes are fun.'

Her mum looked at her sideways. 'What has happened to you, Janey? You've always been terrified of car washes. The thing is . . . oh, that must be Mr Rownigan.'

Janey followed her mum as she got out of the car and went to shake someone's hand. The man was a full two heads taller than her mother and had a mop of sandy hair. When he smiled down at Jean, his soft brown eyes crinkling at the corners, Janey could have sworn she saw her mum sway a little.

'Mr Rownigan, can I introduce my daughter, Janey? I'm just taking her to school. Hope you don't mind her coming along.'

'Not at all,' said Mr Rownigan, shaking Janey's hand too. 'Abraham Rownigan. Delighted. Love children.' He shot a movie-star grin at Janey, and she couldn't help but smile back.

'Janey, Mr Rownigan called last night. He has a proposition about combining our businesses in some way.' Jean Brown spoke in a little rush that made her sound rather out of breath, and she refused to catch Janey's eye as she devoted all her attention to her potential new business partner.

'Please, you must call me Abe,' said Mr Rownigan.

He swept his arm around the yard. 'So, what do you think, Jean? Can't you just see it now? A chain of my car washes, attached to teams of your cleaners vacuuming and polishing the insides, doing all the valeting. I've even thought of a name for it. How about this?'

He whipped something out of his pocket. It was the size of a couple of handkerchiefs sewn together – in fact, realized Janey, it *was* a couple of handkerchiefs sewn together. On it, in marker pen, a few words had been scrawled.

'"Abe 'n' Jean's Clean Machines",' read Jean. She laughed. 'Well, it certainly has a ring to it. But it's not really something I'd ever considered . . .'

No, thought Janey, but then the Clean Jean Company had really been Janey's idea, and not only had it made her mum much happier than she'd been in a long time, it had also meant they finally had some money. 'You should talk to Uncle James about it, Mum,' she suggested. Her mum's brother was something boring in a bank and helped her mum to run the business.

Abe shuffled sheepishly. 'Well, look, I hope you won't think it a terrible intrusion, but I did already have a word with your investors. I'm sure you'll understand that I needed some investigation into a company I might go into partnership with. I only work with the best, and you've done so phenomenally well in such a short time.'

Jean smoothed her overall self-consciously and smiled up at Abe, and Janey felt an odd emotion judder through her. In the embarrassed silence that followed, they all stared at the white car as it edged out of the car wash. There was certainly no rust on it any longer. In fact, the paint sparkled with such a glittering diamond glare that Janey had to shield her eyes a little. The chrome bumper gleamed, the windows were so clean they were practically invisible and the driver put on his sunglasses as bright sunlight bounced off the ice-white bonnet.

'Blimey!' said Janey. 'That looks like a different car! Mum, if you got the insides as clean as the outside, you could make a fortune!'

'Well, I can see you know what you're doing, and I certainly don't hate the idea, Mr Rownigan. Um . . . Abe,' said Jean. 'We'd have to go into it more thoroughly, of course.'

Abe rubbed his hands together. 'Right. Well, look, it's just a suggestion, but how about you and I get together at, say, six tomorrow, and we can thrash through a few martinis. I mean, ideas.'

Janey waited knowingly for her mother to refuse. Friday night was pizza night. The two of them always enjoyed kicking off their shoes, shoving in a DVD and munching on a Meat Feast with extra cheese. But suddenly . . .

'That's a great plan,' said Jean, smiling.

Janey and her mum climbed back in the van and drove jerkily back out on to the main road while Abe stood and waved them off. 'Well, that went very well, don't you think?' said Jean, looking a bit flushed.

Janey was silent for a moment. 'Mum, have you . . . have you just agreed to go out on a date?'

Jean let out a shrill laugh. 'Don't be ridiculous, Janey! It's business, that's all. Purely business.'

Let's hope so, thought Janey. Her stomach seemed to flip. She couldn't let her mum find a new partner. Apart from anything else, although Jean Brown didn't know it, her husband – Janey's dad – was still alive!

french friends

Paulette Solay clung to Alfie like bubblegum to the bottom of a desk, and Janey was finding it rather annoying. When she arrived at school she found Paulette and Alfie in close conference over last night's homework, so she didn't have any opportunity to tell him what had happened to Trouble. At break-time, Paulette bought chocolate bars for herself and Alfie and just about remembered to snap off a morsel for Janey. She couldn't get a moment alone with Alfie, so in the end she resorted to puzzles.

'Hey, Alfie, you know scat rhymes with cat?' Janey said casually as they walked along to the dining hall at lunchtime.

'Huh? Yes, it does. Well done. No, that's the *library*, Paulette,' said Alfie, steering the new girl away.

'You know – scat, cat, rat,' Janey prompted.

'Oh, you like ze rats!' Paulette sidled up beside them. 'I don't know why people have such a problem wiz zem. Zey are very intelligent animals, you know, and—'

'Well, I don't know much about them really,' interrupted Janey. 'It's just that my friend likes rapping, and I was trying to think of something that rhymes with rat and cat, and maybe . . . um . . . *drain.*'

Paulette regarded her with puzzlement, as if Janey had gone completely crazy. Alfie, though, was quick off the mark. 'Train? Take the strain? Brain? Look, I'm just going in here, see you at lunch. No, Paulette, these are the boys' toilets . . .'

Janey shepherded Paulette to a table and got out her sandwiches. She would have much preferred what Paulette was having. First of all the French girl extracted a large croissant from her lunch box. It was filled with ham and melty cheese and some kind of chutney. Next she found a little circle of French bread, smeared with delicious-looking pâté. Finally she added a perfectly round, juicy peach and a couple of squares of nearly black chocolate to the pile.

Janey drooled. 'Is that what you have for lunch in France?'

'Of course,' said Paulette, frowning.

'So did your mum pack your lunch,' Janey asked, fiddling with her dull beef-paste sandwich, 'or your dad?' She was always intrigued to hear about other people's families, having grown up without her dad around.

'No, no. My mother is an international model, Venus Solay, and she is quite often on . . .'ow you say . . . a job? *Non, non,* it is, I zink, assignment. And Papa is in the diplomatic service. The cook gets my lunch. Oh look, 'ere is Alfie. Alfie!' Paulette waved energetically across the hall. 'You can sit 'ere!'

'Thanks,' said Alfie, blushing slightly. Everyone had turned to stare at them.

This was impossible. Janey had to do something to get rid of Paulette for a moment. 'Oh, look, Paulette,' she said, 'Alfie hasn't got a drink. Would you like to get him some water from the fountain over there?'

'Yes!' cried Paulette and scampered off eagerly.

Alfie sighed. 'Bit much, huh?'

'Never mind that,' said Janey. 'I found Trouble in the sewers last night. And while we were down there, someone emptied a swimming pool.'

'Could be from Winton Baths. Or even a private pool? There are some round here.'

Janey's eyes widened in amazement as she grabbed her apple. 'Really? Who would be rich enough to have their own pool?'

'We 'ave a pool!' beamed Paulette, putting a glass of water down in front of Alfie. She'd also got one for herself, Janey noticed. 'Don't you 'ave one?'

'No,' said Janey.

'Perhaps you would like to see it, Alfie. Come tonight. And bring your mother!'

'Erm . . .' said Alfie. The lure of a private swimming pool was too much for him. 'OK.'

Nice one, Alfie, thought Janey, feeling completely left out. 'I'll ask my mum too,' Janey said, although she seriously doubted that anyone cared whether she was there.

'Oh! Of course,' said Paulette, turning instantly back to Alfie.

Janey fiddled with her sandwiches and listened to Paulette's endless chatter. By the time their lunch hour was over, it was a relief to go back to the classroom and start working again.

As it turned out, Jean was not able – or willing – to go anyway. 'I've got that meeting with Abe. Don't want to be late. Sorry, Janey, that means I can't take you over there, or pick you up. And the babysitter should be arriving any moment.'

'Fine.' Janey wasn't even sure she really wanted to go to Paulette's. At least now she had a good excuse. 'I'll be doing my homework in my room.'

Janey shovelled down her casserole and went upstairs as soon as the babysitter arrived and her mother rushed out of the house in an outfit that was a bit too sparkly for a business meeting. It was time to catch up with G-Mamma. Janey pushed through the fireplace tunnel, but the Spylab seemed unusually quiet. 'G-Mamma?'

Her voice echoed off the Spylab walls. 'Trouble? Here, Trubs.' The room felt eerily empty without her SPI:KE or her cat. Janey wandered over to the computer bench and stopped short at the sight of G-Mamma's big clear writing. Janey's own name had been hastily scrawled in lilac nail varnish, with a big arrow pointing to the computer screen. Janey looked at the winking website, puzzled. 'Sunny Jim's Swims. Oh! The water park!'

Did G-Mamma think the water in the drain had come from there? Perhaps she and Trouble had gone to take another look, although it was unusual for G-Mamma to rush off in such a hurry, or take Trouble on a mission with her. There was no time to waste. She left a quick message for Alfie on his phone, coded in case anyone was listening – 'Hope you're having a good swim at Paulette's. I'm going for one myself at Sunny Jim's Swims. My godmother's there, so there'll probably be trouble! You know how crazy she is. Anyway, see you later.' She printed a map off the computer screen, then jumped into the Wower and let it work its magic, smoothing out her hair and her pointy elbows and knees and turning her into Sensational Spylet, Jane Blonde.

As she was about to push open the Wower door, Janey paused. There was a sound – a footstep across the room, at the top of the spiral staircase. Someone had come in downstairs and was headed for the Spylab. It was someone with a light step – so certainly not G-Mamma.

Thank goodness for Ultra-gogs, thought Janey. She sneaked a hand out of the Wower and flicked the light switch. The room plunged into darkness. Her Ultra-gogs switched instantly to night vision, but the figure continued its aproach. Perhaps it was wearing Ultra-gogs too? In which case it had to be . . .

'A spy!' yelled Janey. 'Aaaarghh!' She reached back into the Wower, grabbed the shower head and turned its full pressure on to the approaching body.

'It's me, Janey! Turn it off! And stop bellowing!'

With a gasp, Janey turned off the Wower and switched on the lights. Alfie stood before her in very wet jeans and a T-shirt and wearing, to Janey's surprise, a large boxing glove on one hand. Water dripped off his flattened hair and down his nose.

'Well, so much for me coming over here in my SPI gear, ready to help you. You just de-Wowed me!'

'Sorry!' Janey slammed the Wower shut and handed Alfie a towel. 'I thought you must be a baddy.'

Alfie glared. 'You do know some *good* SPIs and Spylets, you know! Anyway. Look, I got your weird phone message on the way home from Paulette's, so Mum brought me straight round. You're going swimming tonight?'

'No, listen. G-Mamma's disappeared, and I think she's at Sunny Jim's Swims – that water park in Cranwell. Trouble may be with her. She left a message for me, so she must want me to follow her. I've got to hurry,' said Janey, crossing to the computer. 'Do you know how to work a Satispy?'

Alfie paled. 'Don't be an idiot, Blonde. You're not meant to use them yet. Solomon hasn't given them the all-clear!'

Janey typed furiously until finally the computer gave a beep and the word Satispy flashed in front of her. 'Well, I've used one already, and it was fine. Look in that drawer, would you, and find the remote control. Ah, here we go. Footprint.' She tapped in 'Sunny Jim's Swims'.

Alfie was rifling through a drawer, shaking his head like a wet dog. 'You must be mad. They're still experimental. Oh, what a shame, there's no remote control here.'

Janey quickly finished her typing and peered over his shoulder. 'Yes, there is. That's it.'

She whisked out of the house to the back of G-Mamma's garden, pulling on her Girl-gauntlet, Alfie hot on her heels. 'You stay here and sound the alarm if I'm not back by morning,' she hissed.

Alfie looked furious. 'What am I – messenger boy? And anyway, Blonde, you can't use that thing!'

'I have to get to G-Mamma. Cover for me,' was all Janey said as she lifted her thumb to press the remote control.

But Alfie had no intention of standing back and watching his friend take her life in her hands – she could be walking into a trap . . . As Janey pressed the button he lunged forward and tried to wrestle the remote control out of her hand. For a moment he nearly succeeded, but Janey gripped it harder.

'Yowwwwwwwww!' cried Alfie.

Janey stared at her friend in horrified fascination as his body separated into a million tiny particles and streamed upwards towards the satellite dish that could transport them across the world. Alfie had been zapped into space by the Satispy and was now batting about the galaxy in bits before being reassembled back on Earth, hopefully at their desired destination. What Janey didn't understand was how she could still see his eyeball so close by, when he'd obviously just been Satispied and his body was zinging through space. Unless . . .

'Aaaaaaagrrhghghgh!' yelled Janey and Alfie in unison.

Janey's voice sounded very far away. She'd been Satispied too. In fact, they'd been Satispied together. Both Janey and Alfie were whizzing through the atmosphere in a rivulet of cells. Zap! They hit the satellite, and Janey felt the crushing headache that meant they'd finished their upward journey and were now descending. She watched, fascinated, as Alfie started to reappear like a jigsaw before her eyes.

They smacked into the ground and lay there, not daring to move until the shock of their journey subsided. After a while Janey lifted her head to check the Satispy had sent them to the right place. It certainly seemed to have done. The air was thick with the smell of chlorine, and they had narrowly avoided being set down on top of the viciously barbed golden gates. Janey stood and brushed herself off. At least they weren't in a pool. They had touched down on the wrong side of the gates, next to the Coach-Stop Cafe, and a flagpole pointing out where the various water slides were.

Alfie got to his feet, looking a bit green but grinning as if he'd just come off the best fairground ride ever. 'Blonde, that was awesome!' he said, then stopped in horror.

Janey stared back at him. 'Say something else,' she said quietly; then she too clapped a hand over her mouth in shock.

'Crikey, Alfie! Does this mean what I think it means?'

Slowly, as if he could hardly bear to hear the noise coming out of his mouth, Alfie nodded. 'I think we've swapped voices. Oh yuck. Oh yuck yuck yuck. I sound like a girl!'

'That's not the worst of it,' said Janey in Alfie's voice. It almost made her laugh, it sounded so peculiar. 'Look at your right hand.'

Alfie lifted the hand to his face and went white. 'Girl-gauntlet?' he squeaked. 'I'm wearing your Girl-gauntlet! We've swapped hands too! Look, you've got my Boy-battler.'

'I knew there was something funny going on when I just biffed myself in the face.'

'I told you it was too early to use the Satispy, Blonde,' piped Alfie furiously. 'You've turned us into freaks!'

It was true. Janey inspected her left hand. It was much bigger than normal, with thick, stubby fingers. She felt as if she had frying pans at the ends of her arms, and no matter how hard she tried she couldn't get the fingers to work. Her right hand was encased in a huge boxing glove, which just wobbled around on the end of Janey's bony arm. Alfie looked equally ridiculous with a slender little hand protruding from one sleeve and a Girl-gauntlet sticking out of the other.

'There's not much we can do about it now,' said Janey in her new, deeper, sarcastic voice. 'We've got to find G-Mamma. Let's get over the gates.'

Janey looked at the sign she could see gleaming above their heads – a vast, improbably golden sun beaming down from the top of a water slide on to some joyous children, with the slogan 'Sunny Jim's Swims – where Sun is King!' 'We'll bounce over the top.'

'I haven't got my Fleet-feet on.' They both looked at his dripping trainers, relieved to see that they hadn't swapped feet as well as hands and voices.

'Oh,' said Janey gruffly. 'Well, what do you suggest?'

'Just give the gate a whack with my Boy-battler,' said Alfie, crossing his arms sulkily. 'I'd do it myself only you've got my hand.'

Janey stared at the boxing glove. 'OK,' she said and swung her arm back. It felt weird, and she would far rather have been lasering a neat hole through the metal with her Girl-gauntlet, but the Boy-battler did the trick. As it made contact with the gates the glove quadrupled in size and stuck like glue to the metal surface. When Janey wriggled her hand around it stayed stuck, but on the second wriggle a disc of metal the size of a dustbin lid detached itself from the glove and dropped on to the concrete at her feet in a soggy mass. The glove immediately shrank back to its regular size.

'Acid sacs,' said Alfie in his odd high voice. 'Works every time.'

Janey had already jumped through the hole in a neat forward roll. Alfie clambered through after her, and together they looked around cautiously at the selection of toddler pools, spa baths and rippling water slides that winked inkily in the moonlight.

'Anything?' whispered Alfie.

Janey shook her head. An odd silence, heavy with anticipation, mingled eerily with the gentle lap and hiss of the water.

'There's nobody here,' Alfie said, splashing through the paddling pool. His words, in Janey's voice, echoed around them. 'We'll have to think again.'

Janey waded across the pool to join him. 'It does seem pretty empty. Let's check the offices.'

But just then Janey heard a series of blood-curdling snarls behind her and realized her mistake.

'Oops,' said Alfie-in-Janey's-voice.

They turned around slowly, back to back. They were surrounded. Closing in on them was a pack of ferocious, snarling vermin.

'What are they?' hissed Alfie.

'They're rats,' said Janey. 'Enormous ones – could be water rats. Maybe this is what the message on the classroom window was about.'

The biggest water rat was hunkering down on to its haunches, and the others followed suit, all looking ready to use their teeth. As the smallest water rat leaped towards them, Janey lifted her right hand to stun-gas it, but felt only the clumsy weight of Alfie's Boy-battler. 'No stun-gas?'

Alfie was staring with similar confusion at the Girl-gauntlet. 'No, just hit it!'

The vicious water rat was sailing through the air towards Janey's throat. She formed a fist and the Boy-battler filled instantly with compressed air, doubling in size and weight so that Janey felt as though she had a brick resting on her knuckles. She drew back her arm and walloped the airborne creature on the nose as it opened its predator jaws; to Janey's delight the water rat yowled and sailed back into the churning wave pool.

But there was no time to celebrate. In seconds the animal was back up again, while another was rushing at Alfie's ankles. Alfie was trying ineffectually to kick out at the creature while fiddling furiously with the Girl-gauntlet.

'Little finger, stun-gas!' hissed Janey, lashing out at another water rat making a dive for her arm. Alfie squeezed the Girl-gauntlet clumsily with his left hand, to be rewarded only with a tiny click and flash.

'No, that's the camera! *Little* finger!' Janey batted away another snarling creature, with a super-sized thumb in its eyeball.

'I know. It's your stupid hands – they don't work.' Alfie tried again and managed to find the right digit; a tiny blast of gas squirted out into the face of his attacker. It dropped to the ground, right in the path of a fourth rat, which was slavering after Alfie like a rabid bulldog. The rat tripped, yelped as it fell over its companion and crashed into a low wall. It had hardly hit the floor before it was up again.

'Watch out, Blonde. These rats just keep on coming!' shouted Alfie.

The fifth and final water rat was treading towards them more cautiously. It might have been easy to handle on its own, but the other creatures had recovered remarkably quickly and were shaking themselves down, quivering and snarling with rage as they raced towards Janey and Alfie.

Janey looked around desperately. They were trapped. Behind them were the lockers, row after row of open-doored metal cupboards. The gate with the hole in it was too far away. There was nowhere to run.

'We'll have to tackle them, then make a run for it!' shrilled Alfie, dropping down into a fighting position.

'No!' said Janey, sounding very stern in Alfie's voice. 'This way.' She stepped backwards towards the lockers.

Alfie squeaked in frustration. 'But we'll be trapped!'

'Trust me,' said Janey.

As soon as their retreating feet touched the metal edges of the lockers, Janey turned her back to Alfie and linked her arms through his. The water rats were ten metres away. It seemed as if the Spylets would feel their flesh part from their bones at any second.

'Jump!' yelled Janie.

In the same split second, Janey and Alfie jumped. Janey hauled her legs up as close to her chest as she could, then rammed her feet into the ground. She had to work for both of them. With a dull thud and a flare, her Fleet-feet exploded into action. Janey hung on to Alfie with all her strength as they both rose several metres into the air.

The water rats shot under their feet, looking up and howling with rage as they realized that their

43

momentum was carrying them straight through the open metal doors. They couldn't stop. As the Spylets began their descent towards the ground, the water rats piled into the back of the lockers like cars on a foggy motorway. Quick as a flash, Janey and Alfie hit the ground, grabbed a door each, slammed them closed and turned the key.

They held up their gloved hands and, over the howls from the lockers, did a clumsy high-five. 'Cool!' squeaked Alfie.

Janey giggled. 'We have to find G-Mamma and get these voices sorted out! But first we'd better try to find out where our ratty friends came from.'

'I saw one pop out of the spraying tree thingy in the middle of the toddler pool.' Alfie marched through the water and pulled at the fake palm tree that rose from the tropical island. Nothing happened. 'Use the acid sac again.'

'No, look,' said Janey, peering at the trunk of the tree. 'There's a button.' It was tiny, and tucked away under a leaf, but there it was – a little golden button, a miniature sun, glistening invitingly. 'Too high up for the toddlers, but just right for me if I stretch a bit more.'

She pressed the tiny sun and watched in amazement as the island shifted instantly to one side and a large Perspex cylinder appeared by her feet. 'There you go. Looks like a Spylab entry cylinder to me.'

Janey ignored the caterwauling of the trapped water rats and stepped into the cylinder, quickly followed by Alfie. They rode downwards, standing on a fat cushion of compressed air, and moments later they rolled out into a vast underground laboratory.

'What is this place?' said Janey. She dropped down as Alfie dived behind a counter. Anyone could be lurking there.

'It's a Spylab, isn't it?' whispered Alfie.

'Must be. But it's the biggest one I've ever seen. And it's all . . . black.'

They looked around. The Spylab was cavernous. Six long benches stretched out across the room, so dark they looked as though they had been cut from the night sky. Smoky glass cupboards lined the walls; a gleaming ebony door hid a freezer, judging by the temperature gauge on the wall beside it; and screening off one corner of the room was a huge bank of television screens. The blackness was oppressive. The only things that brightened it at all were the golden sun emblems embossed on to every surface.

'Weird.' Janey checked her Ultra-gogs for movement. Nothing. 'G-Mamma, are you here? Where are you?'

'Alfie?' G-Mamma's own voice sounded muffled and distant. 'What are you doing here? We're in the corner, behind the TV wall.'

The two Spylets ran to the screens, but paused when they noticed the images projected on to a dozen or so of them. They were all photographs of Trouble – Trouble in mid-air; Trouble with whiskers like icicles, shivering and glaring malevolently at the camera; Trouble going through an MRI scanner, with the images of his brain scans flashing up beside it.

Someone had been doing experiments on poor little Trouble! And what was that glinting on every picture . . . ?

'Hurry up, Spylet! Get me out!' yelled G-Mamma.

Janey and Alfie followed her voice and then stopped short, colliding into each other. Ahead of them, Trouble, sopping wet and with great clumps of tawny fur missing, was trapped like a fish in shoulder-high water, behind a large pane of toughened glass. Beside him bobbed G-Mamma, resplendent in knee-length flowery bloomers, a Day-Glo green swimming top and a magnificent bathing hat that resembled a rosebush. Two plastic roses formed the large pink goggles from behind which her round eyes blinked at them.

'Oh, G-Mamma! Trouble!' Janey sped over to the glass. The cat miaowed at her pathetically. 'What happened? What's been going on?'

'Sweet Solomon! What has happened to your voice?'

'We swapped,' said Alfie.

G-Mamma's eyes bulged. 'Satispy?'

'Yep, but never mind that.' Janey rattled the pane of glass, but it didn't budge. 'Who put you in here?'

'Hoped you might know, girly-girl! There was a squabble in the garden, and I ran out just in time to see this bunch of giant rats herding Trouble into a Sunny Jim's van. I took off after them like a flying spy. I only just had time to leave you a message.'

'And it was a trap?' asked Alfie.

'Noooo, I just felt like a paddle, Halo. And being like a balloon, I always have to tie myself to the bottom of a fish tank in order to take a dip.' G-Mamma, rolling her eyes, nodded at the chain anchoring her to the floor of the tank. 'Of course it was a trap! And I waltzed straight into it. I hate rats! I was backed into this tank and pinned down before I could say Solomon's Swanky Swimmers. Thank goodness I changed before I came. Couldn't find my Fleet-feet though so I had to wear these.' She waved her free foot around in the water for Alfie and Janey to see the little wheels popping out of the heel of her red biker boot. 'Skates. That's why I wasn't quite balanced when they rounded up on me, nasty little . . . yeuch. Anyway, puss and I have been trying to get out for the last two hours, but can you find a diamond-tipped glass cutter when you need one?'

Janey gasped. 'Hold on just five minutes.' She opened the freezer door and stepped inside, switching the thermostat down as she went. A couple of minutes later she heard piercing, verminous shrieks coming from above.

'Get your booty out of there, Blonde. Someone's coming,' cried G-Mamma.

Janey peeked through the freezer door. G-Mamma was thrashing around madly, Trouble was frantically pawing the water and Alfie was crouching out of sight behind the wall of television screens.

Then, as the water rats exploded into a cacophony of wails, a menacing robotic voice rattled down the entry-cylinder tube to the Spylab: 'Ding dong bell, pussy's in the well. Who put him down? Little Janey Brown.' A blood-curdling metallic laugh rang out. 'So, Blonde, you'll have discovered there's no glass cutter to be found – and that's the only way to get them out. You have to let the cat out of the bag, if you want your kitty and that useless SPI:KE to live. Stay right where you are!'

'Halo,' hissed Janey through the thick freezer door. 'I just need another thirty seconds. Keep them talking!'

It took a moment for Alfie to realize what she meant, and then suddenly he called out in Janey's voice, 'All right! Don't harm them, please. Erm, who are you, sir? Has someone . . . er, sent you?'

'The Sun King answers to nobody!' thundered the voice.

'Sorry!' said Alfie quickly. 'Course not, Mr . . . er . . . Sun King! I'm waiting right here until you come down. I'll tell you anything you need to know. Just don't hurt my cat . . . Oh, or my SPI:KE either, obviously. Just tell me what you want!'

Clever, thought Janey. The robotic voice seemed to scratch the sides of the cylinder on the way down. 'It's simple, Blonde. We want the cat's secret.'

Alfie looked over at Janey as she hovered just inside the freezer door. She shrugged. Trouble had quite a few secrets, but which one did this Sun King mean? The fact that he was a Spycat? That he used to belong to Solomon Brown? That he detested mice? 'So, you mean, uh . . .' said Alfie-as-Janey, playing for time, '. . . um, the secret of all cats?'

The Sun King laughed, and Janey shivered at the

sound. She closed the freezer door as much as she could, to keep the cold in without losing her view of the tank and Alfie. 'Come along, fool! Stop stalling. You need to tell us the cat-creation secret – how Brown turned a frog into this pitiful little pussycat. I have seen for myself that is what happened.'

Janey was too bewildered to answer. She knew her dad had turned a frog into a mouse. That had been the biggest discovery of his spy life – the key to turning one life form into another. But that had nothing to do with Trouble. Surely Trubs had always been 100 per cent pure kitty-cat.

Suddenly there was a small beep near her eye. The gauge on her Ultra-gogs read minus fifteen degrees. Janey had waited long enough. She took a deep breath, wrenched open the door and Fleet-footed across the immense Spylab.

'I want to see your miserable faces when you tell me the secret,' said the Sun King in his grinding tones. 'Or when you see your godmother and your little cat . . . drown. His nine lives can't help him now I've got him trapped in the tank!'

Janey rolled across the floor to Alfie. 'Actually we do have a choice of glass cutters,' she whispered. 'You get ready to laser G-Mamma's chain apart – ring finger on the Girl-gauntlet – and I'll tackle the glass.'

Janey grabbed her frozen ponytail and pointed it at the tank. She carefully scoured the tip of her hair down the glass; there was a hideous scratching sound, then Janey stood back and high-kicked the tank. The glass shattered cleanly and Janey pulled the bedraggled Trouble through gushing water for the second time in two days, out of his prison. As water cascaded around him Alfie directed a narrow red beam of light at G-Mamma's ankle, sliced through the chain and stepped smartly to one side as the SPI:KE flopped to the floor beside him.

Struggling to stand on her wheeled boots, G-Mamma seized Trouble and the Satispy remote control from Janey. 'Trouble first,' she said, positioning the cat under a skylight. She pressed the remote control with an orange-tipped talon. 'Then you, Blonde.'

'No, you next, G-Mamma. I'll go last.' Alfie took the control, pointed at G-Mamma, and pushed the button. At the same time he yelled out to the descending Sun King. 'Yes. Right. I'm going to wait here until you come down. I can't bear to see my little cat get hurt. I am just a poor defenceless girly spy. You can have the cat secret you need, just promise to let G-Mamma and Trouble go free . . .'

Janey grinned as Alfie turned the control to her and pressed it again. As her body separated she could just make out Alfie turning the control around to aim at his own chest. He launched himself into the stratosphere just as the long black soles of a pair of shoes appeared at the bottom of the entry cylinder. 'Got to go, sorry!' he squealed.

Minutes later they all touched down in G-Mamma's back garden, colliding under a rowan tree.

'Good work, Halo,' said Janey. 'Yes! I'm me again.'

'Me too,' said Alfie, inspecting his chunky hands with delight.

Trouble ran over to Janey, and she hugged his wet, scrawny little body. 'Glad you're back, Trubs.'

But relieved as she was, Janey was frightened. Trouble didn't really have nine lives, and he'd never been a frog. How could the Sun King have seen the transformation 'with his own eyes'? Whoever the Sun King was, he knew where Trouble – and Janey – lived, and he was convinced they knew something of value. He was obviously ruthless – prepared to kill. She was going to have to be a lot more careful in future. And a whole lot more suspicious of everybody. Or at least anybody new.

the scare-taker

'Project work all day today!' said Mr Saunders the next morning, stifling a yawn. 'Yes, thought you'd be thrilled. I'd like you to get into work-groups of three and find out as much as possible about one of our natural resources. You'll present to the rest of the class next week. Presentations are to be original and exciting, please. I'm just popping out. No rowdiness.'

Janey got into a huddle with Alfie, trying not to be irritated that Paulette instantly assumed she could join them. After last night the Spylets had a lot to talk about.

'That's a bit un-boring for Saunders, isn't it?' said Alfie.

'Well, we might as well make the most of it,' said Janey. 'What are we going to do our project on?'

''Ang on, I am squeezing my lemon.' Paulette stared intently at the ceiling, her small tanned chin wrinkled in concentration.

Alfie squinted. 'Huh?'

'I get it,' said Janey. 'We call it something else here –

racking your brains. Or, you know, working something out, or . . .'

''Ow about water?' said Paulette directly to Alfie. 'It is our most important natural resource, is it not? Wizout it we die.'

'True. And sometimes wiz . . . I mean, with it we die too,' said Alfie, glancing at Janey.

Janey had to admit it was a good idea. Water was cropping up a lot recently in her secret spy life. She had nearly drowned in the tunnel a couple of nights ago. Trouble and G-Mamma had been up to their ears in it the previous evening. And the Sun King's Spylab was under a water park. 'Maybe we should look at where water around here comes from?' she offered.

Paulette jumped in with yet another idea. 'Yes, and we can find out who uses ze water too. Alfie, what is it you sink?'

'Good ideas, team,' said Alfie in Class Superstar mode. 'We'll do a consumer survey – who uses the most water and when and stuff. We'll look at where it comes from. And then we'll look at how it gets from the supplier to the consumer. How about that?'

'Ees brilliant!' sighed Paulette. 'We can ask Maman about using water when you come round for a swim tonight. And you and I can go to ze library now to research.'

Janey raised her eyebrows. 'Hello? What am I meant to do?'

Suddenly Paulette gave her a smile that lit up

her small face. 'Janey! I am sorry. Bad Paulette. I take away your friend. You go wiz Alfie, and I will do a survey on water-using around ze school.'

Janey felt a little sheepish. She didn't want Alfie to think she was a wimp. 'No, it's OK,' she said slowly. 'I mean, oh all right. Whatever you think.'

Alfie shrugged as if he didn't care either way and strolled off towards the library as Paulette gave a little wave and trotted in the opposite direction. Janey watched for a moment, trying to decide which way to go, then, on an impulse, she hurried after Paulette. The French girl had stopped next to the water fountain and was asking a few pupils something. They laughed, delighted at her accent, and gave her some comments which she jotted down. Then Paulette moved along the corridor and into the dinner hall. Janey watched as she approached a dinner lady, pointing at the sinks. The woman threw her hands up in mock despair and chatted for a few minutes to Paulette, who nodded seriously and scribbled some notes on her pad.

Janey was about to go over when she saw Paulette nip out of the dinner hall and stop outside the caretaker's cupboard. The caretaker was a pretty big water user, it was true. But Janey watched, confused, as Paulette looked left and right, opened the cupboard door and stepped inside.

Janey approached quietly. She could hear nothing but the tinny sound of a radio playing. Just as she was about to press her ear to the door, the handle turned. Paulette was coming out! Flattening herself against the wall, Janey tried to become invisible, but she was still standing there, bug-eyed, when Paulette opened the door.

'Janey! What are you doing 'ere?'

'I . . . wanted to help!' said Janey, burning bright red.

Paulette fixed her with a strange look. Was it . . . pity? Then she smiled warmly. 'Janey, that ees very kind. See, I zought zis cupboard was a lavatory! Because I was zinking, lavatories take a lot of water, do zey not?'

Janey paused. The door did have a toilet-y look about it. But the cupboard was pretty small, and it wouldn't have taken long to figure out there was no toilet in there. Paulette was staring at Janey expectantly, so she said, 'Yes, they do! Great thought, Paulette. Let's go . . . erm . . . interview someone in the actual toilets. How often do you flush? That kind of thing.'

Paulette giggled as Janey, thinking what a stupid thing that was to say, turned even brighter scarlet. Just like the old Janey Brown. She put down her head and scuttled after Paulette, just happening to catch the look that the French girl threw along the corridor to the retreating back of someone who was walking towards the caretaker's cupboard, the light glistening off his bald head.

It was Mr Saunders.

As soon as Janey got home she left a message on the Hallidays' answerphone, filling them in on Paulette's strange little trip to the caretaker's cupboard – and her sighting of Mr Saunders going in to the very same cupboard moments later. Hopefully Alfie would keep his eyes peeled for anything suspicious at Paulette's that evening. Janey slammed down the phone and leaped up the stairs two at a time. She closed her bedroom door carefully and crept to the fireplace, pushing on the point on the wall that operated the sliding panel. She was about to drop to her knees to wriggle through to G-Mamma's when she heard her SPI:KE squeaking in fear.

'Now stay back. I'm warning you, I am a fully trained combat expert. And I could always just sit on your fluffy furry little bones!'

'G-Mamma,' whispered Janey along the tunnel, 'what's going on?'

'Blonde, close the panel, quick!' shouted the SPI:KE.

Janey surged backwards as fast as she could, but not fast enough. Two pairs of eyes gleamed at her from the depths of the fireplace; as she stood up there was a ferocious snarl and a pair of water rats flew past her ankles and bumped into the bed.

Janey turned, horrified, as the animals spun around and came at her again. She was still in her school clothes, with no Girl-gauntlet or SPI-buys to turn on them. The first water rat was rushing at her, teeth gnashing. Janey grabbed a huge encyclopedia from the mantelpiece and swung at it. The heavy book bounced off the water rat's shoulder and the creature dropped, yowling, to the floor. Janey threw the encyclopedia at it with as much strength as she could summon. It landed on the water rat, squashing it flat to the carpet. 'Gross!' said Janey out loud.

Through the tunnel she could hear G-Mamma swatting at the other animals.

'Think you can get me, huh?' she was calling. 'Fancy a piece of Groovelicious G-Mamma, huh? Well, you just try it, little water-ratty-face! Bring it on, you sad little snifflers!'

Janey heard a couple more thumps and venomous cries – G-Mamma was clearly holding her own. But now the other water rat was circling Janey. It coiled, low to the floor, growling in the back of its throat. It was taking its time, sizing her up, before launching a terrifying attack. Janey was completely defenceless. Any minute now the vicious creature would lunge at her, and with her back to the fireplace she had nowhere to go.

Except . . . Janey knew what the water rat was thinking. She could see it looking for her most vulnerable spot, the place that would hurt most as it sank its teeth into her. Slowly Janey bent over, looking as anxious as possible, and covered her bony knees with her hands.

It was a bluff. Much as she hated her knees, they were not her most vulnerable spot. The water rat, however, was fooled, and lunged for them. Janey slapped as hard as she could on the wall above the fireplace and fired her body through the open tunnel like a human cannonball, just ahead of the rat. She whacked the button on G-Mamma's side of the tunnel and the metal plate slid towards the floor. Janey whipped her feet out of the way of the door as it slammed home, but the rat was not so fast. It howled, thrashing madly. Janey had to turn away as the metal ground down on to the creature's body. When the parts of the rat she could see had finally stopped wriggling Janey opened the door again, flung the body by its worm-like tail back into her bedroom to join the other on the floor and scrabbled backwards into the Spylab.

G-Mamma was doing a little celebration dance around the scattered debris on the Spylab floor. 'We kicked their little rat behinds, oh yeah. Oh yeah!'

'G-Mamma, are you OK? Where are they?'

'Scarpered!' G-Mamma rolled her hips in a victory shimmy. 'Ran away when they saw what they were up against! Just when I was about to lock them in the freezer too. How'd you get on, Blondette?'

'I . . . I think I killed them both.'

They were silent for a moment, and Janey couldn't stop her eyes filling up. The rats might be evil vermin, but she didn't want to be a killer.

'You did what you had to do, Spylet,' said G-Mamma. 'They'd have done the same to you, mighty all-righty.'

'But what were they doing here?'

G-Mamma pointed to where Trouble sat shivering under a workbench. 'Looking for Trouble again. They'd backed him into a corner when I found them.'

Janey sighed. 'I don't understand why they think they can learn anything about Crystal Clarification from him. Why can't they just leave him alone?'

'Hmm,' said G-Mamma gravely. 'Who knows how they've even found out *anything* about Solomon's work. I don't like it. Evil's close again, Blonde. We have to let your father know what's going on.'

'But I haven't heard from him – and I've no way of getting in touch.'

'Nobody at SPI has heard from him either, but don't you worry, we'll track him down,' said G-Mamma, flicking on the kettle. 'Now, that was a bit of a shock, wasn't it? Think we need some hot sweet tea and a Fondant Fancy or three.'

Janey shook her head. 'I'd better go and move those bodies before Mum sees them. She'll have a fit if she finds dead rats in the house. Could you do a search on the Sun King for me?'

'Sure. I want to find out about that Spylab anyway. Maybe shut it down. Now don't you worry about the cakes – I'll eat yours for you.' G-Mamma popped a Fondant Fancy into her mouth. 'Let's debrief in the morning. Good way to start the weekend.'

Janey nodded and pushed back through the tunnel. She would have to put the dead water rats in her SPI-buys box and bury them in the garden later – not something she'd look forward to at the best of times, but especially not in the dark, when more murderous animals might be lurking. On her elbows she shuffled forward into her room, dreading what she had to do.

But the sight that met her was even worse than she was expecting.

Janey gulped.

They were gone. The dead water rats were

nowhere to be seen. Only the fallen encyclopedia gave any hint of the fracas that had just occurred, and as she felt a cold breeze ruffle her hair Janey saw their means of escape. The window was wide open. The other three animals must have climbed in and pulled the bodies away.

This is really weird, thought Janey.

If only she could get in touch with her father he would know what to do. But she didn't have a way of contacting him – right when she needed him most.

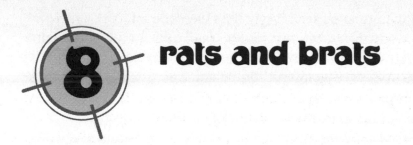

rats and brats

Janey got up on Saturday to find her mother already sitting at the table, fully dressed. 'Good morning, darling!'

'Morning, Mum,' said Janey cautiously. 'You're up early.' Her mother was not known for being at her best first thing. Janey didn't trust the eager look on her face, or the way she was gushing.

'I know! I've no idea where all this energy is coming from. But Abe wants to go through some more ideas. We're very keen at Clean Machines! Oh! Sounds like a slogan, doesn't it?' Grinning, Jean waved the newspaper at Janey. 'Anyway, just time to read this before we get picked up at nine.'

Janey hardly dared to ask. 'Where are *we* going at nine?'

'Well, Abe thought it would be a good plan for us to do a tour of the area and check out what car-wash facilities there already are. And then we can have lunch out in the country somewhere.'

Janey did not want to go. There was too much to

do. She had to debrief with G-Mamma. She needed to talk to the Hallidays. Most of all, she had to find a way to get in touch with her father and warn him that the Sun King was after Trouble and had a team of evil water rats as back-up. Oh, and she'd better tell him that his beloved wife was looking very mushy over another man. 'You don't want me getting in the way, Mum. Why don't I see if I can spend the morning at Alfie's?'

'What a good idea!' said her mother, rather too quickly. 'You're right, of course, it would be very boring for you. We'll drop you on the way. Now I must iron my new top.'

With a sigh, Janey walked into the hall and picked up the phone. 'Hello, Mrs Halliday, it's Janey. Is it OK if I come round today? Mum's going out. Yes, it will be great to have a good long chat with you and Alfie and . . . well, *anyone else who might turn up.*' Janey knew that her SPI:KE had tapped the Browns' phone and hoped she would pick up the message and meet her at the Hallidays' underground Spylab.

As Janey put the receiver down there was a smart rap at the door behind her. Through the glass panel she could see Abe Rownigan lurking tentatively on the doorstep, and as she opened the door he held out a small gift-wrapped parcel.

'For you, Janey!' he said. She took the package, confused. 'Sort of . . . an apology for monopolizing your mum a bit. And something for you to do in the back of the car today when we're nattering about business things.' He looked at her anxiously. 'If you've already got one, I can change it for something else.'

Opening the packet, Janey cast an eye furtively over Abe Rownigan. He seemed pleasant enough. Janey almost felt sorry for him – he had no way of knowing that Jean Brown's husband, who was meant to have died a decade ago, was actually still alive and still in love with his wife – and still the only dad that Janey would ever want. She smiled brightly and focused her attention on unwrapping her gift.

'Oh, wow! An iPod!' Janey went pink with pleasure. 'No, I haven't got one of these – they cost a fortune, don't they? But . . . I probably shouldn't take it. I'm not even coming with you today.'

Looking disappointed, Abe shrugged. 'Oh, well, I was . . . you know . . . looking forward to getting to know you, Janey. I think it's important we all get on, with your mum and me about to go into partnership. But never mind. There'll be other times. And of course you should keep the iPod. I hope you like my musical taste too – I've recorded some things on there.'

'Thanks, Abe. Thank you very much,' Janey stammered.

'Don't mention it.' He started to smile, but was interrupted by a thrashing sound from the bushes. Suddenly Trouble launched himself from the hedge and jumped up on to Abe's thigh. He tried to shake the cat off but Trouble hung on determinedly, trying to climb up his jacket.

'Trouble!' Janey collared the cat and yanked him off Abe. 'I'm so sorry. Maybe . . . maybe it's because you're so tall. He might think you're a tree.'

'Ha, yes, a tree! Easy mistake to make!' Abe guffawed, but Janey thought she caught him glaring at Trouble as he walked up the hall.

'Janey, is that Abe?' Jean Brown was glowing in a rose-pink top. 'We may as well get going, don't you think?'

'After you,' said Abe. Wreathed in smiles, he pointed to a large shabby car. 'Excuse the dirt. I thought it might look peculiar turning up at a car wash in something immaculate.'

Janey clambered on to the cracked leather seat in the back and turned on the iPod as her mother and Abe chattered happily. To anyone outside it must have looked like a happy family outing, thought Janey. She switched up the volume as a new song began: 'Isn't she lovely?' sang a man into her ear. 'Isn't she wonderful?' Janey couldn't believe it! Abe was letting her know what he thought of her mother! Angrily she ripped out the earphones and shoved the iPod into her pocket, then muttered goodbye as she jumped out at Alfie's house.

'Are you all right, Blonde?' said Mrs Halliday as she opened the front door. 'You look quite sick.'

Just then G-Mamma raced up the path, a vision in a gold-and-silver kaftan. 'Solomon's sickly swoonies, girly-girl. Just saw your mum drive off with a very yummalicious man. What's that all about?'

'That's enough, Rosie,' said Maisie Halliday. 'Come on in, everybody. We'd better start talking.'

They all trooped down to the Halos' Spylab under the stairs, gathering around a polished steel table in the middle. Mrs Halliday assured them that they could leave checking out Mr Saunders to her.

'And as for Paulette,' said Alfie, 'the caretaker's cupboard does look like a toilet from the outside.'

Janey glared at him. Now he was starting to stand up for Paulette instead of taking her side. 'Well, it doesn't from the *inside*. It shouldn't have taken her five minutes to work it out.'

Alfie just shrugged as G-Mamma slapped a hand on the table. 'Never mind all that for now. What's going on with your mother?'

Janey told them all about the meetings and plans with Abe Rownigan. 'And now he's even buying me presents to make me like him,' she ended, throwing the iPod on to the table.

Mrs Halliday and G-Mamma looked at each other. 'Are you thinking what I'm thinking?' they said in unison.

Mrs Halliday turned to Janey. 'Looks like a SPI-Pod to me – a SPI-Position Orbital Detector. They're made to look like an ordinary iPod. Only a handful of top spies have them – they're still in development.'

'You can use it to tag people,' said G-Mamma. 'or to listen in on their conversations.' She pulled off one of her large silver wedge-heel shoes. 'As long as you have this on you, Janey, that Abe character can pinpoint exactly where you are – and hear exactly what you say!' And with that she heaved the shoe above her head and thumped it down on the SPI-Pod. It cracked into two pieces, both of which were set upon by G-Mamma's new hammer. 'Well. That. Takes. Care. Of. That!' she said, whacking with each word.

Janey was speechless. Abe had meant to spy on her!

Mrs Halliday smiled gently. 'You'll have to look out for Abraham Rownigan, Janey. For your mother's sake too.'

'Shh!' said Alfie suddenly. 'Someone's outside.' He indicated a small red light that was blinking on and off on the control console beside them.

'Onions with bunions! Look out there in your vegetable patch!' shrieked G-Mamma. She peered into a large chrome periscope above the table. 'Well, if that doesn't just prove it. He planted the SPI-Pod on you, for sure, to lead those evil little weasels right to us.'

Janey snatched the periscope from G-Mamma and gazed at the view in the Hallidays' garden. 'But . . . but that's not possible. There are five of them!'

'Perfect, Blonde!' said G-Mamma, taking a shoe in each hand. 'One each for you guys and two for me.'

But Janey had turned white. 'G-Mamma . . . Halos. I killed them. I'm sure I did. Last night, two of them were definitely dead.'

'There must be more of them,' said Mrs Halliday sensibly.

'No, it's the same ones,' said Janey. 'Look, the big reddish one and the one with a bit taken off its tail.'

'You must have just knocked them out,' said Alfie, reaching for a button, 'or maybe they were faking so they could escape. Put your clodhoppers down, G-Mamma. You won't need those today.'

Janey watched through the periscope as Alfie flicked on the water sprinkler system, then turned up the pressure until each jet was like a water cannon. The water rats were hit from every direction, blasted painfully in the ribs, face, tail. Over and over the jets ricocheted off them. After a couple of minutes of bedlam, all five fled. Alfie was right – Janey must only have stunned them.

'Better keep these to hand,' said G-Mamma, brandishing her shoes. 'Don't want those things attacking me on the way home. I'm going to go and do some more investigation into Mr Rownigan and the growly old Sun King – you never know, they might just be one and the same person.'

'Right,' said Mrs Halliday, getting to her feet, 'and I'm going to do something about our defence system. I don't want those creatures turning up in the bedroom at night. You two can debrief,' she finished, looking at the two Spylets, 'while Al Halo tidies his bedroom.'

'Aw, Mum, come on!' groaned Alfie.

'You're only a Spylet some of the time, Alfie. But you're my son all the time, and my son keeps his bedroom tidy. Hop to it.'

When Janey saw the state of Alfie's room she could see why his mother had put her foot down. Football kit was strewn around on top of magazines, school books and half-eaten bowls of cornflakes. 'Euuww. How can you sleep in here?'

'Don't you start as well,' said Alfie. 'It's not my fault the last cleaners turned out to be psycho killers.'

Janey picked up an exercise book on which Alfie had written: 'Project'. The pages were completely empty. 'So what did you find out about Paulette?'

'Well, not much.' Alfie piled some clothes into a thick wad and stuffed them under the bed. 'Bet she doesn't have to tidy her own room though. They're pretty rich. Nice pool – we had a good swim. Then Clod the cook made us tea and drove me home. Excellent steak-frites.'

'Clod the cook? And that's all you found out?' said Janey crossly. 'That they're rich and eat nice food? What about the weird stuff in the caretaker's closet?'

'You're just touchy about Paulette,' said Alfie, sorting speedily through his CD collection. 'Stop being so sensitive. She invited me round again later. You can come if you want.'

Janey dug her hands into her jeans pockets. 'No, thanks.'

She knew when she wasn't wanted. And anyway, she had some investigating to do. She knew, deep down, that she hadn't been mistaken about the water rats being dead. Just as she knew she wasn't imagining the happy look on her mother's face as Abe Rownigan drove away, or the way Trouble had pounced on him. She was being intuitive, not sensitive. It was what Jane Blonde was good at.

a room with a broom

'Anything about the Sun King?' shouted Janey over the sound of the Wower.

'Oh yes. Apparently,' said G-Mamma's voice, crackling into the cubicle, 'it was the name given to a king of France who ruled for a really long time.'

'So he was a French king, was he? *French?* Interesting! I want to check out three things, G-Mamma.' Jane Blonde stepped briskly out of the Wower and pulled on her Girl-gauntlet. 'First, that caretaker's cupboard. Secondly, the Spylab at Sunny Jim's Swims. And third, Abe Rownigan. He's tall enough to have written that message on the window at school, he's spying on me with that SPI-Pod, and he's trying to get very close to my mum. Oh, and Trouble attacked him. He's never done that before.'

'What about the weird robot-voice?'

Janey raised an eyebrow. 'G-Mamma, you're the one who taught me about disguising your voice. He probably just speaks through something – yes, now I think about it, he carries those big hankies around in his pocket. He probably uses those to muffle himself.'

G-Mamma whirled around with a large photo of Abe in her hands. 'Well, according to the Internet he started cleaning cars as a teenager going round on his bike, and now runs this chain of car washes. A good spy could invent that cover, of course. If he is the Sun King, maybe I should come with you.'

'I'll travel faster on my own.'

G-Mamma nodded. 'OK. Take Trouble though. He might be able to point out some clues. And he looks like he's ready.'

Janey laughed as the cat appeared out of the Wower. Trouble looked magnificent, with the gold stripes in his tawny coat glinting and his eyes flickering emerald green. He stalked past Janey with a flick of his quiff and sat down by the door. It was clearly time to go.

'SPIder? Girl-gauntlet? SPIV?' asked G-Mamma. Janey nodded. 'Well, you'd better take this too. You've got a lot of ground to cover.'

'A skateboard?' Janey went grey. 'I can't use one, G-Mamma. I never even mastered my Rollerblades.'

'Blonde, have I ever let you down? Well, yes, OK, I have, but forget about that for now.' G-Mamma put the narrow board on the floor like a platter of clear jelly, and stood on it. Instantly a little pillow of air lifted the board a few centimetres off the floor. 'It's not just a skateboard. It's an ASPIC – Aeronautical SPI Conveyor. Like a biddy little personal hovercraft.' Just to demonstrate, the SPI:KE pushed one foot down at the back. The ASPIC zipped around a few corners of the Spylab before bringing G-

Mamma back to Janey. 'Easy-blue-cheesy, Blonde. Just need to remember, it likes to be within a short distance of the floor. I mean, if I can do it . . .'

'All right, I'll take it,' said Janey, not at all convinced.

'And you can't fall off,' said G-Mamma. 'Your Fleet-feet are automatically magnetized to it. Safe as Sol's Lols. And it straps to your leg when you're not using it. Go get 'em, Blonde-girl!'

Fastening the slender ASPIC around her thigh like armour-plating, Janey whistled gently to Trouble, and the three of them made their way outside. 'It's pitch-black out here!' hissed Janey.

G-Mamma pointed to the Spycat. 'Send Trouble ahead. He'll light the way.'

It was true. The glow from his tail was as bright as torch-light. Janey took off on her Fleet-feet, bounding along in great strides that Trouble had no difficulty in matching at first. When he started to slow, Janey picked him up. It was exhilarating, pounding along through the crisp night air with her cat at her side, his quiff waving in the breeze. Before too long the iron railings around the school grounds appeared ahead of her. Janey kept running, stamped her feet hard into the ground and sailed over the railings as if they weren't even there. In seconds the Spylet and her cat had reached one of the back entrances to the school.

Suddenly, Janey found herself standing in a pool of white light. 'Security lights! Oh no! That means any minute now the . . .' There it was, a wailing shriek

71

that bounced off the trees. '. . . alarm will go off! Quick, Trouble, into the trees!'

They scooted backwards as quickly as they could, just as the door opened and a tall figure was silhouetted against the glare of the security light. Janey heard the caretaker curse quietly as he stepped out of the doorway, hesitated and then made his way to the back of the building.

'Now's our chance. Come on!'

They ran stealthily to the perimeter of the semicircle of light, then sprinted at full tilt through the door. The school looked different, more threatening somehow, with the shadows of the night stretching far along the corridors. Trouble seemed to feel it too and slowed to a nervous walk.

Janey shook herself. 'Come on, Blonde. This is your own school!' She led Trouble quickly to the caretaker's cupboard and went to open the door. 'Oh no!' It was padlocked. Janey crouched down and studied the lock. She could laser it, but it would take a long time to get through the solid metal. She picked Trouble up. 'What should I do, Trubs?'

The cat bristled beneath her hands. Someone was coming – and she was exposed in the stark corridor with nowhere to hide. Just as she was deciding that they'd better run, Trouble reached out his front leg and unfurled his paw. A huge, glimmering gold claw curved out of the fur like a miniature pirate's sword; in a matter of seconds, Trouble had whipped it through the padlock, slicing the metal loop in half.

'Wow! What is that, Trouble? A Spycat sabre? Brilliant! We're in!'

The cupboard was just as she remembered – small, messy, smelling faintly of disinfectant. The little silver radio was still playing quietly to itself. 'You're listening to golden oldies,' crooned the radio announcer, making Janey jump. She grinned at her own overreaction, but then leaned in to listen more closely. There was a humming sound buzzing along under the tune from the radio. 'Bad reception,' thought Janey. Once more, there was nothing more suspicious than a couple of wet buckets, a row of mops and brushes and some rubber gloves.

At the end of the corridor, a door slammed. The caretaker was coming back. Janey whirled around in the cupboard, about to push open the door, but the caretaker's footsteps were drawing closer. There was no way she could get out without him seeing her.

'Behind the mops!' Janey whispered. She tugged feverishly at one of the handles to make a hiding place for herself and Trouble – and gasped.

The wall behind the mops was sliding away! In a flash, Trouble slalomed through the mop sticks and pelted through the gap in the wall.

'Trouble, no!' There was no way of knowing who, or what, was behind that wall, and the gap wasn't yet wide enough for Janey to get through. The footsteps were approaching fast. Trying to make the gap widen more quickly, Janey wiggled the mop, but to her

73

dismay her jiggling had the opposite effect and the piece of metal slid back to its original position.

The cupboard door opened. Janey turned slowly to face it, bracing herself for the greeting she was about to get.

'What are you doing in here?' said a furious voice.

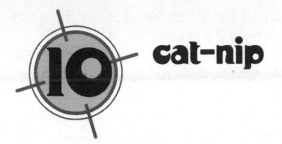

cat-nip

'Alfie!' gasped Janey, so relieved she almost hugged him.

'Come quickly,' said Alfie, stuffing his torch into the pocket of his jeans. 'Good job Mum sent me to have a look round when the alarm was activated.'

Janey grabbed his shoulders. 'There's a hidden room or something behind the wall. Trouble shot inside. We've got to get him out!'

'What?' Bewildered, Alfie squashed in next to Janey in the cupboard and watched as she pulled desperately at the mop handles.

'It won't work! Please work! I just pulled on one of these . . .'

Alfie shushed her. 'I can hear the caretaker coming back. Let's get out of here. We'll have to find another way in.'

Janey nodded helplessly. It seemed to be their only option, even though it did mean leaving Trouble to his own devices. The Spylets backed cautiously out of the cupboard, closed the door as silently as they could and sped off down the corridor in the opposite direction to the steadily approaching footsteps.

'Why aren't you in your SPI gear?' said Janey as they flitted between the bins outside the school kitchens. 'We'd have much more of a chance if you had Fleet-feet on.'

'Who says I'm not wearing my Fleet-feet? This is my SPIsuit, dimbo. You don't think I'd be in all that fussy stretchy stuff, do you?'

Janey looked sideways at him and noticed for the first time that his jeans were part of an all-in-one boiler suit in gently gleaming, soft-as-silk grey denim that bent to his every move. Unlike Janey's suit, Alfie's was covered in zipped pockets that lay to either side of the central zip like the rails on a train track. Some of them bulged, and Janey wondered what manner of gadgetry he had stashed away inside. He had once made a four-seater go-kart out of a suitcase, so she had little doubt that he would have a few life-saving devices about his person. Al Halo looked businesslike and ready for action. 'OK,' said Janey, 'I think we need to double back on ourselves and find that secret room. I've got to get Trouble out.'

Suddenly Alfie stopped short. 'I think Trouble's managed to get himself out.'

They shrank into the shadows as a tremendous din erupted from the school. With a bang, the door flew open. The first silhouette they saw was the caretaker, brandishing a broom handle at a fleeing shadow. *Trouble.* Her cat was haring across the field with his quiff flattened against his head, running so fast it looked as though he would stumble tail-over-nose at any second.

'At least the caretaker will think that was the disturbance,' said Alfie. 'Let's go.'

'No, look!' squeaked Janey, horrified.

Just a little way behind Trouble, five insidious slinking shapes were streaming along like quicksilver, bending and writhing with excitement as they raced after the cat, closing the gap with every second that passed.

Alfie looked amazed. 'It's the water rats again!'

'We've got to save him!' Janey was already off across the school field, barely waiting for the caretaker to close the door behind him. Alfie wasted no time, sprinting after her at high speed. Together they raced across the field, somersaulted over the railings and hit the pavement at full stretch. They ran on towards the high street, following Trouble's bobbing tail.

'Where is he going?' panted Alfie, bewildered, his Ultra-gogs steaming up from his breathing. 'There's only the supermarket and garages down this end of town.'

'I don't know,' gasped Janey. 'Why doesn't he just head for home? Oh, look, Al, they've got him surrounded! Ultra-gogs – zoom!'

The scene ahead of them enlarged so that Janey could make out Trouble's arched back and upright tail, gleaming like a sword. Around him, the five snarling creatures had formed an arc and were moving in slowly. Trouble kept on backing away, into the dark entrance to a large shed-like building. In a panic he scrabbled up the door frame and through an open window, followed by his determined pursuers. But Janey would never fit through.

'You're not going to like this, Blonde,' said Alfie softly. 'Have you noticed what the building is?'

Janey focused her Ultra-gogs. Her heart sank. Across the side of the shed was a slogan she recognized instantly. 'Rownigan's Car Wash – make your car a star!'

'It does say Car Wash, not Cat Wash, doesn't it?' said Alfie, looking around for cover as they approached the shed.

'That's not funny. Poor Trouble must be terrified. At least he loves water. You take the back and I'll go to the front.'

Janey could see now that Trouble had been manoeuvred right inside the car wash. 'Trouble! They're trying to trap him again, Alfie,' she yelled. 'They're going to do more of those horrid experiments on him.' Janey hammered on the door, not caring if the vermin turned round and attacked her – hoping, in fact, that they would, instead of concentrating so single-mindedly on her cat. But the water rats simply slunk back towards the door, looking startled as the great machinery sprang to life.

Janey heard Alfie shouting from the other side of the car wash. 'They've started the cleaning process – it must be automatic when the door's closed. Can you open it at your end?'

Janey ran backwards and forwards along the rigid plastic doors. 'I can't! They're sealed all the way up!'

Trouble had retreated on to the top of a small green car and was sitting on the cream vinyl roof with great dignity as two gigantic sprays swung along on metal galleys over his head. The deluge of water soaked him through in seconds; he shivered slightly and squirmed around as the next stage of the wash pumped into action – the shampoo. A great cloud of foam squirted all over him. Straight across the other side of the car wash, through the foam and steam, Janey could see Alfie trying hopelessly to rattle the doors. He pointed at her ponytail, but Janey shook her head. With no freezer to step into, there was no chance of making a dagger to cut through the thick plastic doors. The only way in was three metres above their heads, where there was a narrow gap between the roof and the top of the door.

Janey tried desperately to remember what came next in a car wash. Trouble was being rinsed and a pair of great blow-dryers was buffeting him this way and that. His hair stood out like a puffball.

Alfie appeared at Janey's side. 'There's no way in round there. And I think he's about to be waxed and polished.'

Janey looked up in horror as six yellow rollers, each the size of a tractor tyre, moved into position ready to buff Trouble into oblivion. 'He'll be crushed! Halo, I have to do something!'

The buffers cranked downwards. Trouble scurried this way and that across the roof but there was nowhere for him to go. The rats were about to have their prey delivered right to them, clean, dry and fluffy. Driven by her cat's fear, Janey sprang into action.

'Why do I do these things?' she groaned, pulling the ASPIC from her thigh and stepping on it.

Alfie watched her, puzzled. 'They don't fly, you know. They only hover above a surface.'

'I know,' said Janey, pushing down on the back of the board. 'But who said the surface had to be horizontal?'

Hoping desperately that the Fleet-feet would stay anchored to the board, Janey floated along the ground, then, holding her breath, she jumped up and flung herself backwards at the same time so that the ASPIC made contact with the vast plastic car-wash doors. It held. She was now hovering a little way off the doors, her body parallel with the ground.

'Wouldn't have thought of that,' said Alfie grudgingly. 'Get on with it then.'

She kicked off again and the ASPIC shot up the door with Janey dangling off it like a zip fastener. She paused briefly at the top, crouching to get through the slot between the roof and the doors, then whizzed noiselessly down the inside of the plastic door, with the floor of the car wash rushing up to meet her.

The big buffer wheels were grinding towards Trouble, who had given up all pretence of bravery and was yowling with heartbreaking volume. He was just a few seconds away from being turned into a small tawny rug.

'Trouble! Here!'

All the creatures in the car wash turned to look at

Janey. The water rats slavered furiously and leaped on to the car, their intention obvious. They needed Trouble. And Janey wasn't getting him back.

But Jane Blonde wasn't about to give up. Just as the rollers descended towards Trouble, Janey pushed off hard on the ASPIC, steadied herself as it lurched horribly to and fro, and lunged towards the car.

The five rats leaped at her from all directions as she skimmed along the roof of the car, the rollers pressing down on her head. Reaching out her arms, she grabbed her wringing-wet cat and sped out through the ever-closing gap, rat teeth snagging at her SPIsuit and furry bodies hurling themselves at her in an effort to knock her off the ASPIC.

She was almost horizontal against the board; Trouble was flat out in front of her like the cat on the front of a Jaguar car; the gap beneath the buffers was closing, closing, closing. Janey shut her eyes . . .

Suddenly they were through. Trouble jumped on to the floor and raced round in little circles of delight. Janey leaped off the ASPIC and turned around as a hideous caterwauling rose up behind her. It was no good. She had to look away. Even though the animals were evil and vicious creatures, Janey did not want to watch them all being crushed beneath those relentless giant buffers.

Alfie opened the door as soon as the car-wash cycle had finished. 'Don't look, it won't be pretty,' he said, steering Janey out of the shed.

Trouble shivered alongside Janey. 'I have to

81

get him home,' she said, kissing the cat's dilapidated quiff. 'That was all a bit hairy. I think we should walk.'

As they began to plod home Janey was deep in thought. 'They're definitely dead now, aren't they?' she said, more to herself than Alfie.

'Oh yes,' said Alfie. 'Unless there's a miracle.'

Something prodded Janey's memory, and a metallic rasping echoed in her head. Perhaps the rats didn't need a miracle. Perhaps they had something better . . .

flying Kites

That night's decode, debrief, de-Wow left a lot to be desired. Janey had more unanswered questions than she had information, and she knew that she had to get a message to her dad somehow or other. Could Abe Rownigan really be the Sun King? What was the mysterious secret the Sun King thought Trouble held? Did the rats have nine lives? She vowed to spend the next day working on it.

But Janey learned the next morning that she and her mother were due to spend Sunday with Abe Rownigan.

'Mum, do you think it's a good idea, working with Mr Rownigan? I mean, you seem to be . . . you know . . . moving ahead with things very quickly. And you don't know much about him at all.' She didn't add that she suspected he might be a spy, a vermin-trainer and a kitty-napper.

Her mother squeezed her hand across the table. 'Janey,' she said gently, 'I know you're worried. But he's a very nice man, and the work proposition makes a lot of sense. As for anything else . . . well, we'll just have to wait and see. It's been just you and me for a very long time, hasn't it?'

'That's not it at all!' shouted Janey. 'You don't understand . . . there are so many things—'

'That's enough, Janey,' said Jean, folding her paper away. 'Let's try and enjoy the day, shall we?'

Janey thought about retorting for a moment, but then stood up rapidly. 'OK. I'll go and get dressed.'

'Fine,' said her mum with a grateful smile. 'Wear something nice.'

Janey barged through to G-Mamma's in a flurry. Her SPI:KE was feeding bits of chocolate croissant to Trouble, who snaffled them up eagerly. 'Just giving him sugar after the shock of last night,' G-Mamma explained through a mouthful of pastry.

'G-Mamma, I have to get in touch with my dad. This Abe Rownigan thing is scaring me. He must be biding his time before he does something awful to me or Mum.'

'Or me!' G-Mamma leaped off her silver stool. 'You're right, Blonde. You must do something. Any ideas how to get in touch?'

'Well, he sent me a letter when he wanted to make contact. Maybe I could do the same.'

'Too slow.' G-Mamma spun the computer screen towards her. 'Try an email.'

'I don't know his address and, anyway, anyone could read his emails.' Janey pondered for a moment. 'But . . .

we think he's downloading stuff from the LipSPICK. Could we put a message on there?'

'Brilliant, Blonde! Type it on the computer and then we can scan it in.'

A tiny fizz of light crackled through Janey's brain. 'A code! Or a puzzle! Right!' Five minutes later she had typed out a message. G-Mamma read it aloud as it plopped off the printer.

> Hi Uncle Sol, how are you? Can't stop – rats, sunk in ground here. Mum's new business. Man, very suspect weather! To tell the truth, to Mum it's trouble. I'm worried about school, unusual. Room for help, Janey xx.

The SPI:KE stared at it for long minutes, sucking her cheeks in and out. 'OK, you win. What the hoody-doody are you talking about?'

'He'll get it.' Janey had every confidence in the SPI leader's code-cracking ability. He was the reason she was so good at puzzles herself. 'I've divided the words wrongly. The clue is "can't stop". It tells him to ignore where I've put the full stops, well, all the punctuation, actually. So it says:

'"Rats, Sun King round here. Mum's new business man very suspect. Whether to tell the truth to Mum? It's Trouble I'm worried about. School – unusual room. For help, Janey."'

'Blonde, that's brilliant. Now I'll just scan it and

whizz it across to the LipSPICK. I wonder how he'll get back to us? We'll have to keep checking for answers.'

'I can't. I'm going out with Mum and Abe,' said Janey. 'I thought about trying to get out of it, but I'd better keep an eye on them.'

G-Mamma tutted. 'That woman's in serious trouble already if she's going out with him again! OK. Maybe I'll try and have a peep around the black Spylab at Sunny Jim's Swims – have a little day trip of my own.'

Sighing, Janey crossed back into her room and rifled through her clothes, settling for jeans and a sweatshirt. As she went down the stairs she heard voices at the door. Abe Rownigan was here.

Janey dropped on to the back seat of Abe's Daimler. She looked around for suspicious cat hairs but could see nothing more sinister than the latest copy of *Business Weekly*. As they drove a few miles to the outskirts of town Abe and her mother chatted easily about business plans and opening days and publicity. Janey almost dozed off, and soon they were pulling up outside an old red coach. It looked very familiar.

'This is Sunny Jim's Swims!'

Jean nodded. 'We're not here to swim, but this diner's supposed to be great and Abe suggested we come here.'

I'll bet he did, thought Janey sourly. She clambered out of the car after her mother. He'd probably try to lure them down to the Sun King's Spylab any minute . . .

'Here we go – The Coach-Stop Cafe.' Abe stood

back to let Janey and her mother climb aboard the converted red coach. 'Looks great, doesn't it? Hope the food's
as good – I'm starving.'

They were ushered to a shiny leather booth and Jean
looked round at the chrome and leather interior as she sat
down. 'It's like an old fifties diner. Look, they even have a
jukebox. Go and put some music on, Janey.'

'Great idea,' said Abe, handing Janey a couple of
pound coins. Janey was convinced he was just trying to get
her out of the way, so she shoved the money in as quickly
as possible and punched a few buttons randomly. As she
returned to the table, her mother was rather coyly asking
a question.

'So have you got any children, Abe?'

'A daughter, from my first marriage, but I don't see
much of her these days.' For a moment Abe looked sad,
then he brightened. 'I bet she'd love this though!'

He smiled at Janey. 'What would you do if you were
your mum, Janey? You've already got a successful
growing business, and then this strange man comes and
asks you to go into partnership.'

'I'd investigate you very carefully,' said Janey, 'and see
how much of a strange man you really are.'

'Janey!' Jean looked horrified.

But Abe held up a hand. 'That's the perfect answer,
Jean. Quite right too. You've got a sharp brain, Janey. I
like people who can think for themselves.'

From the looks Janey was getting from her mother,
she might never be allowed to have another thought

again. Abe Rownigan, meanwhile, was looking at her with such a penetrating stare that she had to look away.

'Sorry, Janey,' he said. 'I was staring. Just wondering . . . you don't look much like your mum. You must look like your dad.'

'I never saw him, so I don't know,' said Janey carefully. It sounded suspiciously as if Abe was trying to delve into her father's history, perhaps even find out where he was. 'He's dead,' she added, to ensure he couldn't ask any more questions.

'I'm sorry.' Abe paused for a long moment, then threw down his napkin. 'Come on,' he said impulsively. 'Let's do something fun. Janey, what do you fancy doing?'

A little thrown by the fact that he wasn't suggesting a trip beneath the toddler's pool and into the Sun King's secret lair, Janey pondered her options. Maybe she could find out something valuable if she spent the whole day with Abe. 'Um . . . maybe a walk on the common?' she said, feigning enthusiasm.

'Yes!' yelled Abe. 'I'll buy a kite! Two kites! No, three – one each!'

They got in that evening after a long day. Janey had had to act pleased for much of it so she wouldn't give anything away. But she had to admit, Abe's pretend personality was pretty nice. Her mum was in real trouble. When Abe dropped them off, Jean Brown stood for quite a while staring at the closed door while Janey busied herself in the kitchen.

'There you go, Mum.' Janey handed her mother a cup of tea. 'Just going to pack my school bag for tomorrow.'

'Thanks, Janey. What a lovely end to . . . well, a lovely day.'

Janey smiled awkwardly and ran upstairs and across to G-Mamma's Spylab. 'Well, that was interest— Halos! What are you doing here?' Janey looked at the three spies grouped around G-Mamma's computer.

'Just wishing you were here, Blonde,' said Mrs Halliday. 'G-Mamma told us about this message you've received from Solomon, but the three of us between us can't work it out.'

'Yes, good news, Blondette. Solly Lolly sent you an email.' G-Mamma pointed to the screen.

Janey sprang towards the computer. 'My dear Janey, can't stop either!' she read aloud. 'All change – drat. Keep quiet – moth! Er, not to worry. How's school? Room here close by. Miss you, new guy! You can say that again! Got to get back – Secret! Love, U. Solomon.'

'Well, we could all read that, Blonde,' said Alfie. 'But what does it mean?'

'I'm not sure of all of it, but it's something like: "*All change – drat.*" I think that means he knows we have an enemy – the rats. Then, "*Keep quiet. Mother not to worry. How's school room? Here close by, miss you. New guy, you can . . . you can say that again? Got to get secret back. Love, Uncle Sol.*" Or "*Love You, Sol.*"'

'"You can say that again"?' said G-Mamma,

peering at the screen as if the words were in Hebrew. 'Say what again?'

'I'm not sure.' Janey looked again at the message. 'New guy. New guy. New guy. Oh, I don't know what it means. Well at least he's close by! How close do you think he is?'

'Not close enough,' said G-Mamma suddenly. 'Look what I spy with my little eye. I don't believe it!'

'What?' said everyone together.

G-Mamma pointed to a large television screen, like an oversized SPIV. The picture on it showed Janey's stairs. And out of the darkness at the top, heading downstairs towards the kitchen, with Jean Brown in their sights, was a five-strong group of snarling water rats.

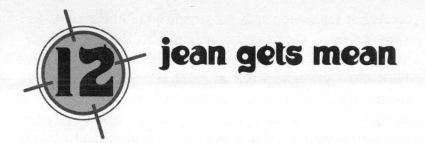

jean gets mean

'Those things are indestructible!' Alfie shook his head in disbelief.

'Look, I've got a theory,' said Janey. 'You know the Sun King has a secret of his own – the one my dad wants to get back? Well, I think I know what it is. It's that these rats have got nine lives, like a cat. I know it sounds crazy – but right now I've got to help Mum!'

While the others took the spiral staircase she scuttled through the tunnel into her bedroom and looked around for a weapon. An idea came to her. Opening her box of SPI-buys, Janey grabbed the bottle of SPIT. She might be able to use it to blind them temporarily while she rescued her mum.

She flew down the stairs just in time to hear her mum crying, 'Oh! Oh, get out, you . . .'

G-Mamma heaved the Browns' front door off its hinges just as Janey reached the bottom of the stairs, and the SPIs and Spylets rushed down the hall towards the sounds of swatting in the kitchen. Jean Brown was standing on the table, batting at the marauding water rats with a rolled-up newspaper.

'What are these . . . these vermin? Euch! Clear off out of my kitchen!' Jean swiped at one with the paper while delivering an effective karate chop to the neck of the other. She looked surprised for a moment, then carried on duelling with her impromptu sword.

'Oh, Mrs Brown, how dreadful!' shouted Mrs Halliday. 'Thank goodness we were calling round.' She picked up a large pan and up-ended it deftly over the nearest rat. There was a howl of rage, and then the pan shuffled around the room until the headmistress put a foot on it.

Alfie grabbed another rat by the tail, swung it round his head and let go. It sailed upwards and landed on the light like a strange fur lampshade, then fell to the floor, singed by the heat of the light bulb.

'Got you, little nasty ratty! Ha!' G-Mamma hoofed it across the room and turned to pull another one off Jean's leg. Jean was holding her own quite admirably, however, kicking and chopping like a karate expert as the two remaining creatures surged around her feet.

Suddenly Janey realized someone was missing from the room. 'Mum, was Trouble in here?'

'Up there,' Jean Brown pointed, swiping vigorously around her knees. 'Came in . . . and . . . vomited chocolate sick . . . all over my cupboard.'

'So he's not here now! Trouble isn't here!' shouted Janey. Suddenly all the rats froze, mid-bite.

'No, I chucked him outside,' said Janey's mum, pointing to the open door with a look of bewilderment.

And with that the water rats took off across the kitchen and broke loose into the garden, all apart from the one that was still trapped in the pan beneath Mrs Halliday's foot.

'Thank you!' said Jean, climbing down from the table with Janey's help. 'What a bizarre thing to happen! Thank goodness you were all here. Er, why were you all here?'

Mrs Halliday patted her hair back into place. 'Alfie and I were just passing. Janey needed to . . . um . . . borrow a book from us.'

'And I heard the screams and just came running! In case it was Janey,' said G-Mamma, looking guiltily at the little pyramid of brown cat-sick.

'Stupid me!' Alfie slapped his forehead dramatically. 'I left the book in the car. Why don't you come and get it, Janey? If you're all right now, Mrs Brown.'

Janey's mother brushed down her skirt, inspecting her legs for teeth-marks. 'Well, amazingly, I'm fine. I don't know where those self-defence moves came from – television, I suppose. In any case, they seemed to do the trick.'

'Gosh, yes!' said G-Mamma, round-eyed. 'Anyone would think you used to be a spy, or something!'

Janey nudged her SPI:KE hard, and signalled to Alfie to grab the rat-filled pan. 'We'll get rid of this last one, Mum. Won't be a moment.'

Outside in the dark, they huddled around the Hallidays' old estate car. 'What are we going to do with it?' said Alfie, prodding at the water rat with a tentative finger. It didn't even retaliate.

'I've got an idea,' said Janey, squirting SPIT over the animal's face. The rat sneezed and looked back at her with bleary eyes. She addressed it firmly. 'You all understood what my mum said about Trouble being outside, didn't you?'

The rat dropped its chin. 'I think that's a yes,' explained Janey to the others. 'You understand what I'm saying?' This time the rat nodded. 'You want Trouble, don't you?' A hasty nod. 'Do you want to kill Trouble?'

This time the rat shook its head.

'You want to do more experiments on him. Why?'

Unlike a human under the influence of truth serum, the water rat didn't open its mouth and start gushing the truth at them, but it did do something almost as strange – it climbed out of the pan, squatted down on its hind legs and bounded around the boot of the car.

'It's having a fit!' yelled G-Mamma. 'Water-ratty mayhem – squash the thing!'

'No,' said Janey. 'It's deliberate. It's jumping like a . . . like a frog.'

As the last word was spoken, the rat turned to Janey and nodded madly.

Janey looked at G-Mamma. 'It's what the Sun King said. They think Trouble was a frog. They want to know more about Sol's secret!' she whispered.

'But how on earth do they know about that?'

'No idea, unless . . .' Janey tried to think. Something was nudging away at her with urgent insistence. Not only was there the puzzle of how the rats knew Solomon's secret, but also something important was escaping her. It was to do with her dad's message too. And suddenly, with a surge of power that made her gasp, it came to her. 'You're not rats at all, are you? You're . . . you're humans?'

With a malevolent gleam in its eye, the rat nodded again.

'Humans turned into water rats. Only one person could have made that happen . . .'

And while they were all looking at each other, dumbstruck, the rat slunk to the edge of the car, slithered to the ground and raced away down the gutter.

'They're humans. Could be spies,' said Janey in hushed tones, unable to move as the shock sank in. 'Solomon used the Crystal Clarification Process on them, and I think he'd only do that to evil spies. So now they want the secret of how to turn back. They need to know the reversal process. And for some reason, they think Trouble is the answer.'

project painful

Monday passed so slowly that it made Janey's skin prickle. With so much to think about, she couldn't concentrate on schoolwork. Who were the rats? What had made her father turn them from humans into animals? And why were they so convinced that Trouble had the information they needed?

It had all rolled around in her mind so much that Janey had a throbbing headache when project time came around. She smiled wanly at Paulette as they gathered together with Alfie around a library table. Paulette beamed back.

'I 'ave been very busy. 'Ere is ze result of my survey. I worked on it all weekend.' Paulette threw a sheaf of papers on to the table, making both Alfie and Janey feel empty-handed and a little guilty.

Janey looked at the name on the presentation – Paulette Soleil. 'So that's how you spell your name. Mr Saunders said it was Solay.'

'Mr Saunders does not know French very well zen, I sink. Shall I put your name on it too, Alfie? Oh, don't worry if you did nussing,' Paulette said, seeing their faces. 'I was just bored because I 'ave no friends after you left on Saturday, and Maman was away all weekend.' She looked helplessly at Alfie.

'Mmm . . . maybe . . . maybe you could come round to my house next weekend,' he said eventually, squirming a little on his chair and trying not to catch Janey's eye.

'Oh, Alfie, 'ow kind! I would love to.'

Janey struggled to join in. 'Was your mum on an assignment?'

Paulette laughed. 'Well, yes, but not ze modelling kind. You see, Maman is also a brilliant businesswoman.'

'So's mine,' said Janey proudly.

'Oh no, it is not ze same. She is very tied up with somesing at ze moment, and she is very, very brilliant.'

'Well, my mum's not exactly stupid!' Janey could hardly believe it. She couldn't stay there with the girl simpering all over Alfie and slighting her mother. 'I'm going.'

'Oh. 'Ave I upsetted 'er?' she heard Paulette ask with not the slightest bit of concern in her voice.

Janey rushed out of the library and down the corridor, shoulders heaving with the effort of keeping her tears locked inside. She was fed up with Paulette treating Alfie as if he was some kind of god.

There was nobody around. And although Mrs Halliday had said she'd check out the caretaker's cupboard herself, Janey thought she might as well have another snoop. She made her way to the cupboard and swiftly entered it.

It only took a few moments to waggle the right broom handle and slip through the gap in the wall where Trouble had disappeared. At the last minute Janey grabbed a bucket and wedged it in the doorway, just in case the door decided to close and there was no way to operate it on the other side. She crept into the secret room, holding her breath. To her surprise, the room was completely empty apart from a pile of pizza containers in the corner – no wonder Trouble had sniffed it out. The only odd thing about it was that the walls were completely covered in egg boxes. She'd been expecting something unusual – maybe even a Spylab – but it was nothing of the kind.

She reached under her jumper for her SPIV. 'G-Mamma, are you there?'

The amber pendant crackled into life. 'Here, Blonde.' G-Mamma's voice sounded oddly serious.

Janey sighed. 'I'm checking out the secret room behind the caretaker's cupboard, and apart from some funny egg boxes on the walls it's completely normal.'

'Well, I've been doing a bit of checking myself,' said G-Mamma. 'Went down to old Jim the Swimster's to close down the black Spylab and found a video playing on a loop. I'm there right now. It's a message. For you.'

'From the Sun King?'

'See for yourself.'

G-Mamma angled her SPIV so that Janey could see the vast bank of television sets that had screened G-Mamma and Trouble from the rest of the lab the last time they'd been there. Each one was lit up by a golden disk in the centre. Janey peered more closely. It wasn't a disk. It was a sun, a vast metallic sun, with slits for eyes and a strange round grille for a mouth – the mask of the Sun King, multiplied dozens of time on the TV wall.

And every one of them was speaking.

'Ding dong bell. Pussy's in the well. Who put him down? Little Janey Brown. You have a cat secret, Janey Brown. And so do I. I'd like to swap secrets with you. You tell me what I need to know, and I will let you in on what I know. But understand this, Blonde. We can do this the easy way – or the hard way. I don't mind. But. I. Will. Find. Out.'

The horrible robotic voice faded as G-Mamma swung her SPIV around and stared at Janey. 'Did you get that?'

Janey gulped. 'He's mad. Completely insane. Get out of there, G-Mamma. I'll see you at home.'

Confused, Janey returned to class, too caught up in what the Sun King had been saying to worry about Paulette any more. She fidgeted until the bell rang, then zipped upstairs to G-Mamma's as soon as she got home.

'This enemy dude has to develop some taste!' yelped G-Mamma as they watched the footage that she'd brought back from the Sun King's Spylab. 'What's wrong with a bit of sparkle, some bling-bling, some pace in your face? Look, how about . . .' G-Mamma leaped to her feet and started clapping like a member of a gospel choir. 'Here goes!

'Ding dong belly, poor pussy's in the welly,
But who put him do-ow-nn? Little Janey Bro-ow-nn.'

Janey slumped over the bench. G-Mamma was not going to be much help today, she could see. 'He's trying to say it's my fault Trouble's in, er, trouble, but I don't see how. Any messages from my dad?'

G-Mamma shook her head. 'Sorry, girly-girl. But good rap . . .

'My girl can't find her daddy
And it makes her kind of saddy
But he is not aroun-n-n-nd
He just needs to be fouun-n-n-nd . . .

'Anyway,' she said abruptly as Janey scowled at her, 'I'm sure Solomon will somehow pop out of the woodwork any minute, but right now we need to give the Sun King what he wants.'

'We wouldn't actually swap secrets, would we? You might have forgotten, but we don't actually know how to change rats back into humans, G-Mamma.'

'What do you take me for, honey-child!? Even if we did know we wouldn't really tell them.' G-Mamma plopped down on to her stool with rosy cheeks. 'No indeedy! Trust is everything in Solomon's Polifrcational Investigations! We'd just *pretend* to exchange secrets, that's all.'

Janey was still wondering about this later as she

peeled the lid off a frozen lasagne and pushed it into the microwave. It seemed like a dangerous game to play. On the other hand, it would bring the enemy – Abe Rownigan perhaps – out into the open. She might even be able to impress her dad by learning something about the nine-lives secret. As Janey tipped frozen cauliflower into a pan of hot water, she suddenly came up with an idea.

It had to wait, though, as her mother sallied in through the front door with Abe right behind her. He was clutching a large bottle of champagne and grinning almost as widely as Jean Brown.

'Hello, darling!' said her mother. 'Abe's just sorted all the paperwork out. The first of the Abe 'n' Jean's Clean Machines chain opens in a couple of days! We've got bubbly!'

Janey forced a smile as Trouble ran in from the back garden and squirmed around Abe's legs like a small furry snake. Abe was trying to ignore the cat. 'Do you have champagne flutes, Janey? We'll need three.'

'Abe! I'll get them.' Jean Brown almost skipped out of the room.

'We don't have any special champagne glasses. Just tumblers,' said Janey moodily. 'And I can't have any, I'm just a kid.'

'So you are,' said Abe, beaming. 'You're just so sensible I find it hard to remember. Well, anyway, maybe you'd prefer this.'

He reached into his pocket and pulled out a

few items at random: the little banner of handkerchiefs he'd made; a twenty-pound note; a little black enamel jeweller's box. 'Nope, none of those. Ah! Here we go.' And he handed Janey a tiny brooch shaped like a kite. 'Reminded me of our great day out!'

It was very sweet – a red and gold kite with a little row of diamonds for a tail. Janey looked up from the glazed, multicoloured surface of the brooch to find Abe gazing at her anxiously.

'Is it OK? It's only a little badge, but it's real gold!' He turned the kite over to point out the hallmark on the back. 'The diamonds are just crystals though.'

Janey went pink. It was the prettiest thing she'd ever owned, but hadn't his last present turned out to be something quite sinister? 'It's lovely,' she mumbled. 'Thank you.'

'My pleasure. Now, how about this champagne? Jean! There you go. To a wonderful venture.'

Abe Rownigan and Jean Brown clinked glasses, smiling at each other. Janey felt as though she shouldn't even be there, with all the grinning and clinking that was going on.

As the microwave pinged, Janey's mum turned to Abe. 'Aha! Dinner! Would you like to stay?'

But Abe seemed in a hurry to be off. He glanced at his watch. 'Thanks, Jean, but we've got an early start tomorrow. Think I'll hit the road. Bye, Janey. See you in the morning, Clean Jean!'

Jean Brown managed to blush, smile and look slightly

disappointed, all at the same time. 'Of course. Early start. See you then.'

Janey watched her mum's face as Abe Rownigan disappeared down the hallway and out of the door. She had to expose him now – before her mum's heart was broken – or worse.

brain strain

There was no point trying to be secretive. For once Janey wanted the enemy to know she was there. G-Mamma dropped her some distance from the gates of Sunny Jim's Swims. 'I'll hide the car and have a snoop around. See if we can get any more clues about this Sun King loon. Holler if you need back-up, Blonde,' she said, revving the engine gently.

'I will,' said Janey. She gave G-Mamma a thumbs-up with her Girl-gauntlet, Fleet-footed to the gate, then, making as much noise as possible, clambered through the hole she had made with Alfie's Boy-battler. Within moments she had activated the Spy entry cylinder in the toddler's pool and rolled into the middle of the glossy black Spylab. The darkness – and the silence – seemed solid.

'OK,' Janey said in a low voice, pulling her Girl-gauntlet more firmly over the items in her hand. 'I'm here. Let's trade.'

For a moment nothing happened, and then suddenly five lithe and loathsome creatures slunk into the room from behind the tank that had held G-Mamma and

Trouble. This time Janey was not afraid of them. She had something they wanted (or so they thought).

The great jagged mask covering the Sun King's face suddenly filled all the television monitors, the voice robotic and harsh. 'You are sensible to trade.'

'Why don't you come out?' said Janey bravely.

There was a hollow laugh. 'You want me to reveal myself? Well, I'm afraid I will not be giving you any satisfaction on that score. But don't think you can escape me. My rats will stop you leaving. Until, of course, you give me what I want.'

'The secret.' Janey tried taking control. 'You have to tell me your secret first. And then I'll tell you mine.'

'No, no, no. First yours. Then we will decide if you are to live or die. Only then will you know our secret.'

For a moment Janey didn't know what to do. If they didn't believe her, she could be in serious trouble. But Jane Blonde knew how to take a calculated risk.

'Fine. I'll go first then.' She pointed at the group of water rats. 'You want to know how to turn these rats back into people.'

Janey tried not to think about the huge chance she was taking. She had to assume that the rats had no real recollection of what had actually been done to them during their transformation.

She took a deep breath. Here goes, she thought. 'So. You start off as one creature, and are frozen, very slowly, until you are solid ice. Then you are turned into some other creature, some other life form.'

'Yes, yes,' the Sun King said impatiently. 'But how is it *reversed*?'

Janey wriggled two little objects out of the cuff of her Girl-gauntlet and caught them in her other hand. As she had hoped, the Gauntlet had kept them chilled and hard. She dropped them on to the palm of the glove and extended her arm.

'Can you see?' she said to the Sun King. The water rats sniffed the air suspiciously.

'Of course. What are they? How are they part of the process?'

'It's what happens next, after the freezing.' Janey forced herself to slow down. If she gabbled too much she might give the game away. 'The top of the frozen head is sliced off. The old brain is removed. And then a frozen brain from the new animal – like this – is inserted into the cavity. It's a brain transplant. As the body begins to melt, the new brain sends out all the necessary patterns and signals along the ner . . . the neurons.' She hoped she'd said that correctly. 'You know how powerful the brain is. It transforms the whole body when it's used as part of this very, very complicated process.'

There was a long silence, as though the Sun King was holding his breath. Finally he spoke. 'Ingenious. Of course. I see how it works. And those things in your hand are . . .'

'Frozen frog brains,' said Janey, holding them higher. 'If you like, we can try them on your water rats.' And she waved the two bits of frozen cauliflower at the creatures.

'That won't be necessary,' snapped the Sun King, as the rats squirmed uncomfortably. A couple of them yowled and snapped at Janey. 'Of course we weren't interested in frogs in general. We just needed to know how to change your cat back into his original life form – a frog – thus all the experiments I conducted. Now we know we merely need to conduct a brain change. Thank you, Blonde. Now all I need are some suitable brains . . .'

Suddenly the danger in the lie Janey had just told hit her. She had to keep talking, fast.

'I see. So you want to change these rats back into people. Well, it's a much more dangerous and difficult process to turn *animals* back into *people*. I don't think it will work. They'd probably die! Reversal has never been tried before.' There was a long silence. Janey took the moment to recover. 'So, I told you my secret. It's time for the trade. You tell me yours. How do you give other creatures nine lives, like cats have?'

She squared her shoulders and tried to look as though she fully expected the secret to be delivered to her right there and then. But the masked face on the screen suddenly tipped back, and a low, vibrating laugh echoed around the lab, getting louder and louder as the Sun King spiralled into hysteria.

'So you worked that out. Well done. But you'll never know the full details of the process, because only my little rat friends have that information. They discovered it, and used it on themselves! But *someone* changed them into vermin before they could divulge the full details. Which is why I need them to be human again – so they can share with me the secret of *immortality*! And now I know the way to create new life too. I am a god!'

Janey felt the panic rising in her throat. She was just a pawn in a far greater game. There was no trade. She had been double-bluffed.

'Silly girl. Why would I trade? You see, now we know that a human brain will transform my rat-spy friends back into their wonderful evil selves. How lucky that we have such a brain, right here.'

'Where?' Janey glanced around but could see nothing that looked like a bigger version of the frozen cauliflower.

'In your head, Blonde,' the Sun King said with venom.

Janey's breath started to come in short little gasps. 'You can't use my brain. It . . . it won't work. It has to be frozen . . . Let me talk to Solomon, or G-Mamma . . .'

As soon as she spoke there was a rattling sound from the top of the entry cylinder. Janey could have kicked herself. She'd only been stalling for time, but of course G-Mamma was nearby with her SPIV activated, waiting for the first mention of her name.

'Stay there! Don't come in!' yelled Janey.

But it was too late; a moment later the SPI:KE rolled into the Spylab in a multicoloured crocheted cardigan and a large peaked cap. She stood up quickly to find five water rats and a very scared Spylet staring at her.

'Good!' rasped the Sun King. 'Two human brains. Time to make some SPIce cubes.'

The mad laugh went through Janey and G-Mamma like an arctic wind.

all fired up

'What are they doing, Blonde?' hissed G-Mamma as the rats formed a ring around them.

Janey, back to back with her SPI:KE, turned inside the circle of rats. 'They're herding us into the freezer. They think they need frozen human brains to turn the rats back into people, and they're going to start with ours!'

G-Mamma started to shake so much it was as if she was doing a dance. 'Outrageous offal! They can't do that! I'm very attached to my brain!'

'Oh, and they won't tell me the nine-lives secret.'

'Evil cheats!' spat G-Mamma as one of the rats lunged for her, forcing them ever closer to the freezer door. She reached out to the end of one of the nearby black benches and grabbed a fire extinguisher. 'Euggh! Don't mess with me, rat-face. I'll . . . I'll foam you to death. '

'They're invincible, remember? But we aren't. We can't let them get us into the freezer,' whispered Janey.

G-Mamma dropped down into a karate pose, which did nothing to frighten the approaching rats. They were now so close that they were snagging her voluminous cardigan with their teeth. 'I hope you've got an idea then, Blondette. Otherwise our heads are going to be split open like coconuts while they extract our beany brainies, and then what will happen to us?'

'I don't think we'll care much by then,' hissed Janey. 'At least they won't bother with Trouble any more though.'

'Blonde, much as I love that cat,' said G-Mamma, 'I would rather it was his furry little bod on the line instead of mine. We need to be quick. The only way out is the entry cylinder. How about I take them on and you make a run for it?'

Janey looked over at the plastic cylinder leading up to Sunny Jim's Swims' toddler pool. 'I couldn't leave you . . .'

The rats were springing at them, all slavering jaws and vicious claws, and Janey and G-Mamma were being forced perilously close to the freezer door. Thread from the SPI:KE's woollen cardigan was unravelling across the floor in a red streak that looked horribly like blood. And just then, Janey had an idea.

'Get ready, G-Mamma,' she said in a low voice. 'We're going out of the entry cylinder.'

'What's the plan?' G-Mamma swatted a nearby rat away, then looked down in amazement as Janey grabbed the flapping strand of wool from her crocheted top and tied it around the ASPIC on her thigh.

'Well, we're not going to the cylinder,' said Janey. 'It's coming to us.'

And with that she ripped the ASPIC from her leg and flung it beyond the plastic entry cylinder. The rats' heads whipped round in surprise; Janey braced herself against G-Mamma's back, their arms linked, and lifted her legs so that her magnetized Fleet-feet were aiming directly at the ASPIC.

The moment it felt the pull from the Fleet-feet, the ASPIC switched course and sped back towards them. The wool, unravelling from G-Mamma's cardigan at a mighty speed, lassoed the entry cylinder in a great loop. 'Hang on to me!' shouted Janey, as the ASPIC strained to reach her feet. The cylinder, slowly but surely, swung around to meet them.

'Now!' yelled Janey, the moment she could see the base of the cylinder facing them. The bowed cylinder creaked as the ASPIC finally attached itself to Janey's feet. Instantly, she crouched down on the board and hovered above the heads of the rats. 'Come on!' she screamed to G-Mamma.

As the rats hissed and yowled, G-Mamma seized the back of the ASPIC and Janey pushed down with her heel. They sailed over the snapping animals and into the entry cylinder, with Janey curled up as small as she could make herself, and G-Mamma streaming behind like the tail of a comet. Seconds later they popped up through the toddler pool. Janey made for the hole in the gate and the ASPIC shot through in a neat glide, then stopped dead with a whip-lashing jerk. Without her magnetized feet, Janey would have fallen straight off. She jumped down and turned around to see what had happened. Her SPI:KE's shoulders were wedged in the opening, and her round blue eyes were popping out of their sockets.

'I'm suckered in here like a champagne cork, Blonde! I can hear the rats right behind.' G-Mamma wriggled helplessly. 'Go on without me!'

There was nothing to get hold of apart from G-Mamma's head. 'I'm not leaving you here! You'll have to push yourself through.'

'My feet don't touch the floor! And this wretched fire extinguisher is wedging me in! Go, Janey!'

'Use it! Use the fire extinguisher,' urged Janey, standing well back. 'Now!'

'OK, Blonde! I just hope you know what you're doing!'

G-Mamma wrapped her knees around the fire extinguisher and pressed the lever. Janey could hear the splash of the rats running through the pool.

G-Mamma wobbled furiously and the whole gate shook. Then she shot out of the hole and along the ground as if jet-propelled, knocking Janey flat.

'You're out! Quick, they're coming.' Janey pointed the stun-gas finger at the first water rat to fling itself through the gate.

'Use your ASPIC, Janey. I've got my wheels. I'll meet you at the car.'

Janey whizzed off while G-Mamma let loose with the fire extinguisher, blasting the rats off their feet with a cannon-load of white foam. When they were up and after her again, G-Mamma rolled the extinguisher at them. They stared at the great thunderous object hurtling towards them and tried to scarper. It was too late. The extinguisher ran straight over them as G-Mamma popped the little wheels out of her boots and speed-skated up to Janey.

They reached the car together. G-Mamma swivelled to a spectacular halt that made the gravel fly. 'Woolly pullies, I LOVE being a SPI! Wiped them out again!'

'It's not over yet, G-Mamma,' said Janey, racing to the passenger door as she looked behind them. 'Nine lives, remember?'

G-Mamma blew a raspberry at the rats as she screeched away in the car.

'Maybe they'd be easier to deal with if they *were* humans again,' said Janey thoughtfully.

'Good point, Blondette,' said G-Mamma as they shot round the corner into the street.

The trouble was, there was only one person in the world that knew how to turn the rats back into humans. And Janey had no idea where her dad was.

mixed messages

The next morning, Janey wrote a simple email to her dad.

'Homework – help needed soon. Janey xxx'

G-Mamma was grappling with some turquoise fake eyelashes. 'I know it's the least of our problems but it's still getting to me: why is this Sun King so convinced that Trouble used to be a frog?'

'It is weird,' said Janey, shaking her head. 'Oh, look, I've got a message back!'

'Your father must have been sitting on that computer.' G-Mamma scurried round to Janey's side to read the email. '"Janey, to get to the point: that type of thing is BIG . . . Afraid can't help. Busy right now. End of special project. In touch soon. Stay well, UNCLE SOLOMON." Now what in the name of Brilliance does that mean?'

'It's not in code,' said Janey, swallowing her disappointment. 'This is just a straight message. He's too busy to help.'

'Better go and get your breakfast,' said G-Mamma gently, nodding to the television-sized SPIV that showed the stairs in Janey's house. 'Before Clean Jean starts looking for you. Look, she's on the phone.'

Janey sneaked back through to her room and went down to the kitchen.

'Abe's a bit tied up,' said her mum. 'He can't be at the car wash first thing as planned. We've got suppliers coming and all sorts, but I've got other cleaning jobs to do first – what am I going to do?' Her mother put down her mobile phone and sighed.

'Since when have you had one of those?' Janey pointed to the mobile.

'Abe gave it to me. For business. Good to keep in touch, he says.'

Janey looked suspiciously at the little gadget. Might it be another SPI-Pod to keep constant tracks on her mother's whereabouts? She would have liked to wrestle it out of her mother's hand and bash it to bits, but decided that would look a bit suspicious.

Jean Brown frowned. 'Where am I going to find a cleaner at this short notice?'

At that moment the doorbell rang. Janey and her mother got to the door at the same time. On the doorstep stood a large woman wearing a knotted headscarf, a hygiene mask, a vast flowery overall and white Wellington boots.

'Can I help you?' said Jean, stunned.

'Can I help *you*? is the question,' said the woman. 'Fleur from Short-Cuts Cleaning Temps here. Wondered if you might be needing any work today? I've hit a bit of a lull.'

Jean Brown stared long and hard at the woman. 'You've done cleaning before?'

Fleur gave a short laugh. 'Show me a woman who hasn't, eh, my dear! I've done the lot. Cleaning, steaming, gleaming. In all sorts of places. That's why I keep the mask on. I could start now if you like. Here are my references.' She handed Jean a pile of papers.

'Well, that's . . . that's great. Amazing references. Cleaning at Buckingham Palace? Wow. Well, you've come at the perfect time. I've just got the supermarket contract, over on Besford Drive. You'll probably need my van for the equipment.'

'Smashing,' said Fleur.

'I'll just get the keys.' Jean raised her brows at Janey and flitted down the hall.

Janey took hold of Fleur's arm. 'G-Mamma, what are you doing?'

G-Mamma tapped the side of her nose. 'Going undercover to suss out this Rownigan guy. Get to the bottom of it.'

'But you're useless at cleaning!' said Janey, thinking of the endless trails of crumbs and jam on the Spylab floor.

'True,' said G-Mamma proudly. 'But I'm very good at spying. And lying!' Her eyes crinkled in a fake beam as Jean returned to the door. 'Drop you somewhere, Mrs Brawn?'

'It's *Brown*. No, that's fine, I'll get a cab.'

'Righto. I'll be off,' she said, grabbing the keys from Jean's hand.

Janey could hardly stop herself laughing at the sight of G-Mamma trying to squeeze herself into the Clean Jean minivan. At the same moment all three of them spotted Abe Rownigan's Daimler coming around the corner. G-Mamma dived into the depths of the van and pretended to be sorting the buckets, peeking out from behind a dishcloth.

'Abe, you made it!' said Jean when she could finally tear her eyes away from the new cleaner.

'Yes, everything sorted. Shall we drop you at school, Janey?' He gave her a funny look. 'Oh, you're not wearing your little kite badge today.'

'No,' said Janey hesitantly. 'It's too pretty to wear for school.' Plus it's probably another of your SPI-Pods, she thought darkly.

Abe was watching G-Mamma's behind wobbling around as she tried to right herself in the van. 'Is that a new cleaner?'

'Er, yep,' said Janey quickly. 'Can we go? I don't want to be late.'

She was actually early. When she got out at school, both Abe and her mum turned to wave at her, and for a moment Janey experienced a strange, sudden pang. She was still standing staring after the car as Alfie came up to her.

'Is your mum still playing happy families?' he said, offering her a piece of bubblegum.

Janey nodded. 'Oh, I don't know, Alfie. But the whole thing is getting really scary. Last night the Sun King tried to freeze me and G-Mamma and take out our brains. We only just escaped. I can't help thinking Abe Rownigan is in on it all somehow.'

'Why else would he plant a SPI-Pod on you? Anyway, right now that's the least of our problems,' said Alfie. 'Have you thought of an interesting and original way to do our presentation today?'

Janey groaned. She'd forgotten all about the water project.

'Paulette!' she called to the small figure ahead of her. 'It's the project presentations today. We're not ready!'

Paulette turned to greet them with a knowing smile. 'Ah, don't worry. I 'ave done lots of work.'

Mr Saunders, looking rather tired, called the groups up one by one. When it was their turn, Alfie and Janey hung back while Paulette walked over to the teacher's desk. On it she rigged up a contraption with a large jug, and a plastic bowl with a ruler shoved through it. 'So this is 'ow we save our water *and* generate electricity 'ere in our town. 'Ere is our reservoir,' she said, lifting the jug and pouring water slowly into the half of the plastic bowl behind the ruler. 'And when ze dam is opened we create ze power.'

With a little flourish, Paulette whipped the ruler out of its holes and water gushed into the other half of the plastic bowl. She ignored the rivulets of water oozing across Mr Saunders's desk from the ruler-holes.

'Top marks, Paulette's team,' said Mr Saunders,

getting out a tissue and mopping up. 'You see, class? An original presentation at last. Although, Alfie and Janey, it was meant to be a group effort, you know? You owe a big thank-you to Miss Solay.'

'It is Soleil, going up at ze end, Monsieur Saunders. French for "sun". And it was a group effort, monsieur,' said Paulette. 'We were like family wiz our project. Alfie did . . . Alfie and *Janey* did all ze background work.'

'Good. Let's move on then.'

Paulette winked at them as she sat down, but Janey was lost in her own thoughts. Paulette's surname meant 'sun'. And hadn't the original Sun King been French too? Maybe she was right to be suspicious of Paulette after all.

reeling abe

Janey's mum collected her after school and brought fish and chips home for supper, along with Abe Rownigan. All through the meal Janey was itching to excuse herself and go for an immediate catch-up with G-Mamma. If Paulette was involved in some way, Janey needed a plan.

'Can I go and do my homework upstairs?' she asked as soon as the plates were cleared. 'Leave you in peace.'

Her mum and Abe looked exceptionally happy at this suggestion, it seemed to Janey. She wasn't even sure they'd noticed her leave, but just as she reached the bottom of the stairs, a hand clamped down on her shoulder. It was such a shock that she let out a small scream.

'Oh, sorry, Janey, didn't mean to scare you,' said Abe Rownigan, looking down at her from his great height. 'I just . . . I just wondered if I might have a word.'

Janey perched awkwardly on one stair while Abe squatted at the bottom. 'I . . . I don't know how to say this really, but I just wanted to let you know that I'm not playing games or anything. I'm deadly serious. You're a smart girl, Janey, I'm sure you'll get the message very soon. Please, you see, I mean to get your mother—'

'Just leave her alone!' Janey leaped up, her heart banging against her ribs. He was deadly serious. He was going to get her mother! 'Leave us both alone!' she hissed. 'I've worked you out. I've told you everything already. I can't tell you what you need to know!'

Terrified, she hurled herself past him down the stairs and ran to her mother. 'Make him go, Mum,' she cried, flinging herself across her mother. 'Get him out of the house!'

'Janey!' Jean Brown didn't know whether to calm down her daughter or placate the man in the doorway.

'I think I'd better go,' said Abe. 'Sorry, Jean, I must have said the wrong thing. Janey, I'm so sorry, I thought perhaps you'd understand . . .'

Jean Brown cuddled her shaking daughter. 'Yes, perhaps you had better go. I think Janey and I need a talk on our own. I'll see you at work tomorrow.'

Janey sat down at the kitchen table, hardly daring to look at her mum's face. There was so little she could explain without going into all the details of her spy life, but she knew she had to say something. 'Mum, I know you think I'm a brat, shouting like that. But there's something not right about Abraham Rownigan. I think he might be out to harm you. Us!'

Her mother put a hand over Janey's. 'Darling, I know what this is really about. And I understand. We've been as close as can be, just the two of us, battling against everything together. I haven't even thought about looking for anyone else since your father died. But Abe Rownigan has suddenly turned up, and you don't like the disruption to our normal lives.'

'But we don't have normal lives, Mum,' said Janey. 'We're not *normal* at all! And what if . . . what if Dad didn't really die? What would he think of you liking somebody else?'

'That's completely ridiculous, Janey,' her mum said sharply. 'Of course he died. Just calm down. I've only known Abe a few days! But I'd like to know him for a few more. And if nothing else comes of it, I am quite determined that our business will go ahead. It could be the making of us, Janey. Promise me you will never, ever have an outburst like that again.'

'I was just trying to save you, Mum,' whispered Janey miserably.

'Let me do the saving round here. I've got years of experience. Just . . . just go and do your homework.'

Janey struggled to fight back a flood of tears as she trod heavily up the stairs. If Abe Rownigan *was* trying to destroy their family, he was going about it the right way. Barely managing to close the door behind her, Janey wriggled straight through to the Spylab and collapsed in G-Mamma's aproned lap.

'My mum hates me,' she sobbed, relating what had happened with Abe Rownigan.

'She doesn't hate you, Blondette,' said G-Mamma.

'She hates *me*, and look what that's like. She loves you. But this Abe Rownigan is a worry. Couldn't catch him out on a single thing today, even though I sneaked up on him as many times as I could. Although I suppose . . . well, I suppose there might have been one little thing.'

'What?'

'Well, there were a couple of times, like when I was vacuuming his car roof, looking busy, that I heard a funny noise. And when I swizzled round I could have sworn he was . . . he was . . . laughing at me.' She blew her nose loudly on her apron pocket.

G-Mamma looked so hurt that Janey didn't have the heart to tell her that the sight of her hoovering a car roof probably would have looked pretty funny to anyone. She dried her eyes and checked the super-sized SPIV. Her mother was still in the kitchen, nursing a cup of tea with a sad, faraway look in her eyes.

'Time for a Wower,' she said decisively. 'Abe's a menace. I'm going to find him.'

G-Mamma nodded, more like her usual self. 'Well, it should be easy. I planted a SPI-Pod under his car. What's the plan?'

'Jane Blonde's going to reel Abe Rownigan in,' said Janey. 'That's the plan.'

dam rats

As Janey neared the point indicated by the SPI-Pod, she slowed her ASPIC by skewing it hard left, then pulled out her SPIV.

'G-Mamma!'

'Here, Blonde. OK?'

'Fine. I can see the car. It's parked on Quarry Road, under the trees opposite a big house. And guess what the name is on the gatepost . . . Soleil.'

'Very interesting! You thought they might be connected, didn't you? Don't go in the house, Blondette; it could be a trap. You're wearing the bait?'

Janey glanced down at the small kite brooch pinned to her silver SPIsuit. The tiny diamonds winked at her in the moonlight. 'Yes. If it's a SPI-Pod, like I think it is, he'll know exactly where I am. And I've got Mum's mobile, just in case. I'll check in later.'

Janey slid past the car. There was nobody inside but she could still hear the faint sound of voices singing. Abe had left the radio on. 'Hmm. Your voice intercom, no doubt,' said Janey under her breath. It didn't worry her. This time she wanted the Sun King to find her so she could prove it was Abe.

'Map,' she said to her Ultra-gogs. Instantly a small 3-D image popped up before her eyes. 'OK. The Sun King seems to like water. Let's head down there.'

At the bottom of the road was the old quarry, which had been transformed into the reservoir and dam that Paulette had demonstrated for their project piece. The trees became more sparse as Janey sprinted along.

There ahead of her was the reservoir. The inky surface stretched for several hundred metres; in the far distance Janey could just make out the glint of the narrow rail that ran along the top of the dam. She checked her pocket – there was the SPIder in case she got into difficulties in the water, and the ASPIC weighed comfortably against her thigh.

Janey sat for a few moments hunched under a bush, wondering what someone would think if they found her there talking to a tiny kite. It felt mad, but there had to be some way to activate the SPI-Pod. Just to be sure, she fished her mum's mobile out of her pocket. 'Hello! I am in trouble. Come and find me!' she said loudly.

At last. In the distance Janey could hear the screech of tyres on the shingled road. She crouched into a tight ball and peeked out through the prickly branches. Headlights from the road were brightening the gloom – not just one set, but two, and much further away Janey could make out yet another set.

'Not good,' she said to herself. Janey had really

expected that Rownigan would come on his own. Now there were three carloads of the enemy heading in her direction.

She flattened herself into the ground, the silver-grey of her SPIsuit perfect camouflage, as the first car shot into the car park. It was Abraham Rownigan's Daimler. Janey tried not to breathe as he leaped out of the driver's seat, looked around speedily and ran towards the dam.

The second car – a large black people-carrier – skidded to a halt behind Abe's. A small figure climbed down from the passenger door, quickly followed by the five slinking water rats that Janey had come to know so well and dread even more.

'We will be too late! 'Urry!' hissed the little running figure.

Paulette! She too had taken off towards a small building at the edge of the dam. The rats swarmed around her feet like eels on a river bed.

The third set of headlights was still too far away for Janey to worry about right now. If she waited to see who it was, she would lose Abe Rownigan and Paulette. She got to her feet silently and hauled out her SPIV as she began to tiptoe towards the small building. 'G-Mamma! They're together – Abe and Paulette. They're heading for some kind of shed near the dam. I'm going in.'

Without waiting for a reply, Janey dropped the SPIV back against her chest and ran around the edge of the reservoir. Chalk flew up in puffs around her ankles. There was a bang as the door to the shed was thrown back on its hinges; for a moment she could see Abe Rownigan silhouetted in the doorway, then he ducked down and disappeared from view. Paulette and the rats screeched through the very same doorway seconds later.

'Bingo!' said Janey. Now she could simply lock them in and call for back-up.

She crept into the bushes beside the shed. Behind her a car engine started up. Janey stood cautiously, tiptoed forward to the edge of the shed and chanced a look in the window. The engine sounds were louder here; Janey could see that the building was like the wheelhouse for a watermill. Levers and handles rose from the floor, and the ground vibrated with pulses of energy from the millions of tonnes of water trapped behind the dam.

Just as she pushed the door into place Janey realized that someone was missing. Abe Rownigan was no longer in the shed! He must have rounded back on himself to catch her. She was interrupted by a deafening screech of brakes and turned to find herself spot-lit against the side of the shed by the full beam of an enormous set of headlights.

'Aargh!' Janey tried to shield her eyes and step to the side but the lights swivelled, following her relentlessly.

A hideous metallic laugh emanated from the car. On hearing it, Paulette came out of the shed. 'Janey!' She sounded very surprised.

As Janey turned the car revved. Ahead of her were Paulette, the water rats and the edge of the dam, and behind her was the Sun King, with shafts of moonlight reflecting off his metal mask.

Once again the vile robotic laugh rose into the air, louder and louder. 'Did you think you would trap my little spy-rat friends, Blonde? Aren't you the one who is trapped? Just a poor little rabbit, snared in the headlights.' The Sun King started to chant. 'Run, rabbit, run, rabbit, run, run, run. Just give the farmer his fun, fun, fun. Rabbit pie, Blonde, that's what the farmer makes. Although there's not enough meat on you to make much of a dish.'

'What do you want?' yelled Janey. 'I've told you everything I know.'

'We want the organ-grinder, Blonde, not the monkey,' snarled the mechanical voice. 'You told us how to turn the water rats back into humans. Now we want the surgeon who can carry out the operation.'

Janey laughed, sounding braver than she felt. 'You know Solomon has gone underground again. I'm not even sure he's alive. You'll never be able to turn the rats back into humans, so you'll never learn the secret to a cat's nine lives. You'll die, just like everybody else.'

At this the robotic voice rose to a shriek. 'I am the Sun King, Blonde! The *Sun King*. The centre of the universe! I can never die. But you can. If we threaten your life, the mastermind behind it all will come to save you. And if he doesn't . . .'

Janey gulped. Far from baiting Abe Rownigan into revealing himself, she'd turned into bait herself. Now Abe had disappeared – and she still didn't know how he was involved. At least Abe isn't the Sun King, she thought – but it was little consolation. She looked around desperately. The Sun King's car was edging forward. Paulette and the rats were right behind her, closing in.

There was only one way to go. Up. Janey turned around so she was facing Paulette and the shed beyond – and jumped. The Fleet-feet exploded and she shot upwards, arching over the top of Paulette and her rat cronies. Quick as a flash, Janey ran into the shed and bolted the door behind her.

Paulette's face screwed up with rage. Janey saw her bark some directions at the rats. Immediately they slithered around the side of the building and fanned out along the top of the dam. There was no escape.

The solution came to her in a flash. She was standing next to the gear shafts that operated the dam. If she could open the floodgates a little, the rats would be caught up in the fast-running water. She chose one of the tall metal shafts at random, gripped it with her Girl-gauntlet and gave a mighty heave. It shifted, slowly at first, and then with a sudden swing. The huge gear wheels filled the air with a metallic noise even more horrific than the chanting of the Sun King. A gurgle and swish in the water beside them grew to a rumble, and Janey turned to look through the window. The first plume of water cascaded over the edge of the dam. It was opening. All along the top of the dam water was spurting, diving, plunging into the reservoir below. Janey watched as, one by one, the water rats struggled to keep a grip on the slippery top of the dam. Then they plummeted over the edge.

Just then she noticed something else – a tall figure trying to stand up on the dam as water rushed beneath his feet. Abe Rownigan. Janey gasped. But she had no time to worry about Abe. The Sun King's car had advanced on the shed and kept pushing, intent on toppling it. As it creaked and leaned drunkenly over the edge of the dam, the water thundered like Niagara Falls into the blackness. When a large crack appeared in the side of the shed Janey grabbed her ASPIC and clambered through it to hover barely centimetres above the churning water tumbling over the edge of the dam.

She acted instinctively, digging a heel into the board. She looked back one last time – and realized three things. The Sun King had driven away; Abe Rownigan, who had been running along the walkway on top of the dam towards her, had missed his footing and been slammed straight over the side; and the shed, which had been teetering on the brink of collapse, had now disintegrated and was toppling over the dam, dragging with it a small car that had raced up in the last few seconds, identifiable only by the dustpan and mop sticking out of its roof.

'No!' screamed Janey. In horror, Jane Blonde toppled into the deluge, under a million tonnes of gurgling water.

19 spi-fly

Crushed by the weight of water cascading down on her head, Janey writhed and spun with the ASPIC still suctioned on to her feet. Every part of her felt dislocated and possessed by some evil spirit: her hand would suddenly fly into her face, or her bony knees into her chest. She managed to grab her SPIder, but the force of the water drove her hand downwards, away from her mouth.

It was hopeless. She tried one last time to shove the SPIder between her teeth, but succeeded only in tugging at the tiny diamond ribbon on the bottom of her kite brooch. She was going to die. A black muggy cloud descended over her. Strangely enough she almost felt tranquil, and then she remembered that people who have nearly drowned often say that there is a moment of true calm. Any moment now she would see a bright light at the end of a tunnel and find herself floating towards it.

And there it was – the tug of an angel as Janey's life ebbed away. She was being pulled up through the water by silken wings, beating their way upwards and across the torrent with such force that she had to hold on to the angel's fingers as hard as she could. Janey's eyes closed as the sweet pull dragged her . . .

Then she opened her eyes again. She had definitely just breathed in some air! And these were not angel's wings but a great white sail that had anchored itself between her feet on the ASPIC while her hands held a crossbar that was keeping the sail upright.

'It can't be!' she gasped. 'This crossbar looks like . . . the pin on my brooch!'

She dared to look around. She was still racing down the side of the dam, but now she seemed to be sailing *across* the surface of the water instead of tumbling under it. Far behind her she could see slivers of wood bouncing through the spray, and the unmistakeable sloganed car door of a Clean Jean van.

Janey tilted her weight to the tail end of the ASPIC, instinctively leaning back on the crossbar and swinging the enormous sail around, away from the thundering water. Without warning she was lifted a couple of metres into the air, then used the sail's momentum to hurtle back across the dam, traversing the water like an Olympic skier slaloming down a vertical run. Several times she leaped and turned, until soon she was able to kite-surf across the surging waters at the base of the dam, chancing a somersault as a large wave rose to meet her. The ASPIC came to a shuddering stop above the roof of the Clean Jean van.

'Mum?' she called, kneeling on the board and peering in as far as she dared. 'G-Mamma?'

Both doors had been ripped off, and the little van was empty apart from buckets and a couple of dishcloths. Had the driver been able to jump out and save themselves – or had the water sucked them from the car?

'What have I done?' Janey whispered.

She could not bear it. Every time she had tried to be clever she had put herself and other people into danger. And now she was practically a murderer too. Janey was no less of an evil monster than the Sun King.

Feeling sick, she pointed the sail towards the edge of the lake and made her way, bucking and bouncing across the waves, to the shore. As the ASPIC hovered across the fine chalk-white sand, Janey jumped off, letting the sail sink to the floor. As it hit the sand it instantly started to fold from the top. The bar she had been holding slid in on itself like a telescope until it was the size a brooch pin again. Meanwhile the sail concertinaed into a series of diamond shapes, folding in half repeatedly until it rested back on the pin, just a little gold kite brooch.

Soberly Janey pinned it back on. Abraham Rownigan had given her this brooch, and it had saved her. Why would an enemy do such a thing? Had she managed to kill a friend, not a foe, while allowing the real villains – the Sun King and Paulette – to escape? Janey would have liked to weep, wail and thrash her legs on the floor, but after a few moments she sat up with the very strong sense that she was not alone. A rustle in the trees confirmed her suspicion; instantly Janey was on her feet, brandishing her Girl-gauntlet.

'Put your glove down, Blonde. Do you want everyone to see? Have I taught you nothing?'

'G-Mamma!' Janey didn't care who saw as she ran into the bushes to where her SPI:KE lay, wet and with smeared make-up, but most definitely alive. 'Was Mum in the van too?'

'Nope. Tucked up at home watching *CSI*,' panted G-Mamma.

Janey threw her arms around her SPI:KE. 'I didn't kill you!'

'Nice try though,' coughed G-Mamma. 'I thought I was a dodo when I set off from that great height like *Chitty Chitty Bang Bang*, only without the wings.'

'How did you escape?'

G-Mamma spat delicately, and a fluorescent orange SPIder flopped out of her mouth into the undergrowth. 'I had time to chew my SPIder as I flew through the air, then when we hit the water I kicked the doors out and used a couple of mops as paddles. Rowed as far as I could, then swam the rest of the way. I am *pooped*!'

'G-Mamma, that was sheer brilliance!'

'Well, I came hightailing it after you because you said Paulette and Abe were together. I thought you might need assistance.'

'I got it wrong. I'm pretty sure Abe and Paulette weren't together. He went over the dam. It was the Sun King driving that big black car.'

'Well, when I saw what was going on at that shed I had to try to ram that black monster,' said G-Mamma. 'Then I suddenly found myself taking off. But I wasn't the only one. Look.'

Janey followed her finger and gasped. A small raft, made out of debris from the demolished shed, was floating away across the lake. The rats' wet pelts glistened in the moonlight.

'How do they do it?' asked G-Mamma.

'I don't know, but they do look a bit battered, don't they? Maybe they're running out of lives. And why aren't they just swimming – they're water rats, aren't they?' Janey watched them with narrowed eyes and suddenly remembered something. 'Come on, G-Mamma, we've got to get back to your Spylab.'

'Are you suggesting I walk in these heels? You destroyed your mum's little Clean Jean machine.'

'We'll have to take Abe's car,' said Janey. 'Quick.'

G-Mamma rode the ASPIC, and Janey Fleet-footed around the lake and up through the forest to the car park. Once G-Mamma had hot-wired the Daimler and positioned herself lovingly behind the steering wheel, SPI:KE and Spylet raced off into the night.

'There,' said Janey back in G-Mamma's Spylab, pointing to the photograph. 'Alfie took it by mistake when he was trying to stun-gas the water rat at Sunny Jim's Swims on Thursday.' One of the water rats was curled round in a ball, protecting itself from a heavy landing.

G-Mamma pressed her nose against the computer screen. 'Why's it all slimy-looking? Hmm. Well, it looks as though it didn't hit the ground properly. It's swivelling round to land feet first. That could be the secret. You know cats always land feet first.' She peered around the Spylab. 'There you are,' she said. 'Come on, Twubbly Wubbly. I want to try something.'

Trouble leaped on to the countertop, expecting his usual helping of cuddles and petting, only to find himself brushed off it again by a well-padded arm. He landed lightly on all four of his mini-lion paws and stalked off angrily with his tail in the air.

'See, did you notice? He turned over and landed on all fours.' G-Mamma beamed at Janey.

'But the water rat in the picture isn't on all fours. It's curled up in a ball. A shiny ball. Why's it all shiny like that?'

G-Mamma shrugged. 'We're going to have to find out pronto-monto. What good is an evil spy that you can't get rid of? Oh, sounds like a car outside.'

Janey scurried to the blind-covered window and peeked between the slats. 'Someone's pulling up in a Clean Jean van. Two people: one short, one tall. Cleaners, I suppose. They're getting out. Now they're walking to Abe Rownigan's car. They're getting in. There's some sort of argument going on. Right, the tall one seems to have won. They're driving . . . G-Mamma! They're driving it away! Quick!'

'Stop panicking, Blonde. I arranged it all,' said

G-Mamma. 'We couldn't let your mum know we've ruined her precious van, could we? I got a replacement. And what if Abe Rownigan is currently reporting his car missing and it's found here? Just covering our tracks, Girly-girl. The agent is driving the Daimler back to the car park at the reservoir.'

Janey giggled. 'Oh! I've just realized who it was. That was Alfie trying to drive the Daimler.'

'Might have been,' said G-Mamma, trying to look mysterious. 'Crazy driver, that Al Halo.'

Takes one to know one, thought Janey.

G-Mamma pointed to the super-sized SPIV, which showed that Jean's bedroom door was starting to open. 'Brekkie time for Blondey. See if Paulette's at school and don't take your eyes off her if she is. Check in later.'

Janey pushed through the tunnel and came to an ungainly stop on the carpet next to her bed. The bedroom door creaked open just as the SPI panel closed behind her.

'You didn't sleep there all night, did you?' said Janey's mother.

'No. Yoga!' said Janey, waving her legs around and pointing her toes.

Jean Brown folded herself gracefully to the floor and took hold of Janey's hand. 'I don't suppose either of us slept too well after last night. I'm sorry, Janey.'

'I'm sorry, too. You don't hate me then?' said Janey quietly.

'I love you, silly.' Her mother got to her feet with the same balletic elegance with which she'd sat down. 'And you're quite right. I'm rushing things with Abe . . . with Mr Rownigan. From now on it's strictly business.'

Janey wished it could be just business for her too, but she had to go to school. She was still thinking things through when she got the message to meet Alfie and his mother in the headmistress's office.

'Paulette is absent today,' said Mrs Halliday. 'No big surprise after last night. So what are we going to do about Abe Rownigan?'

'We have to find his body,' said Janey. 'He gave me a SPI-buy that saved my life. We have to find out exactly who he is. Maybe he gave me the SPI-Pod so he could keep tracks on me – and *help* me. He might even have information on my dad.'

Mrs Halliday rubbed her hands briskly. 'I'll make some calls. You two go to the reservoir and see what you can find.'

The Spylets nodded and left the school quickly. 'I'm sorry I didn't trust your instincts about Paulette. I won't let you down again, Janey. Give me two minutes to Wower, yeah?' said Alfie.

'It's all right, Al. I didn't exactly have much proof before. Now, get changed – quick. I've got my SPIsuit on under my uniform.'

Janey waited impatiently in Alfie's room as he Wowed down in the Hallidays' Spylab. After a couple of minutes Al Halo entered the room, smart and competent-looking in his denim SPIsuit and silver-framed Ultra-gogs. He pulled a blue ASPIC from a cupboard and fastened it on. 'Which way shall we go?'

Janey pulled a face. 'The underground route. I reckon the pipes must lead to the reservoir, and we can't chance being seen. Have you got a SPIder?'

Alfie showed her the gum he was putting in his pocket. 'Off we go then. Down the sewers. Nice.'

He led her to the manhole behind his house and tugged the metal cover aside. 'Which way, Blonde?'

'Map. Reservoir,' said Janey to her Ultra-gogs. Images flickered before her eyes, the pictures getting bigger and more detailed until there was a tiny beep, and a red light appeared over a photograph of the reservoir. 'This way,' she pointed. 'Follow me.'

With Alfie just behind her, Janey zipped through the pipes, bending almost double in places.

'The Ultra-gogs show we're just under Quarry Road. Nearly there . . . Aha! Let's slow down,' said Janey. 'I can see daylight ahead.'

The Spylets cruised to a stop. Fixing the ASPIC around her leg, Janey stepped towards the source of the light and then drew back against the wall of the tunnel.

'We are very, very high up,' she said slowly. Wind whipped her platinum-blonde ponytail back and forth across her head. Cautiously she poked her head out of the end of the tunnel again and peeked upwards. Just above them was the rail that ran along the edge of the top reservoir. Splinters of wood from the shattered shed were just visible too.

Alfie looked down at the huge drop beneath their feet. 'I bet water normally gushes through this tunnel as an overflow for the top reservoir, but it all ran out into the lower reservoir when you opened the dam.'

Janey felt sick. 'I can't believe it. So the wall of water I kite-surfed down last night must have been this high. I had no idea I'd fallen so far.'

They were at least a hundred metres above the water, trapped in a hole in the mighty dam wall. Janey hardly trusted her feet to keep her upright.

'We have to get down,' said Alfie. He pulled at his belt.

'How?' Janey asked.

Alfie clipped the buckle to a hook in the top of the tunnel similar to the one Janey had threaded her hair through when she rescued Trouble. 'It's a SuSPInder. Retractable long rope, to you and me. We're going to abseil.'

'I can't,' said Janey, squashing herself against the curved tunnel wall as Alfie prepared to throw himself over the edge.

'Well, unless you have a magic carpet, we're all out of options.'

Janey's head whipped round as something in the distance caught her eye. 'Focus!' she rapped to the Ultra-gogs. 'Zoom!' She stared at a small figure running along the edge of the lower reservoir. 'Paulette!'

Alfie wrapped the SuSPInder around his waist and started to ease himself over the edge. 'Come on then, let's go after her.'

'There's no time, Alfie, we'll lose her. And besides, I think . . . I do have a magic carpet! Hang on to my feet!'

As quickly as her shaking fingers would allow, Janey unpinned the tiny kite brooch from her SPIsuit. 'Please work!' she yelled and tossed it high into the air.

Janey held her breath. Had she just thrown a SPI-buy to the bottom of a reservoir, or was her instinct about to be rewarded? Suddenly the wind caught the brooch and sent it spinning upwards. Janey grinned as the sail unfolded, over and over, and the pin expanded into a crossbar. The sail floated above them like a great white eagle.

'Ready?' she yelled to Alfie, thrusting her face out into the buffeting wind. 'Catch me!'

Janey leaped out of the tunnel, arms windmilling as the sail filled with air above her. She reached out with one hand and managed to take hold of the crossbar. The sail pitched; Janey threw up her other arm and slapped her other hand into position.

'Jump, Halo!' she called to Alfie. He hesitated for just a moment, then lunged for her ankles. Wildly the Spylets dipped and swerved in the air, then Janey adjusted her grip, turned the nose of the sail towards Paulette and let the wind take them.

'Ha! You've got a SPI-fly! This is fantastic!' yelled Alfie from beneath her feet.

Janey's face was contorted into a weird gummy smile by the pummelling wind. She could feel with the instincts of a bird how the breeze billowed this way and that. As the sail tugged, Jane Blonde allowed it to cast itself into the best currents, and in just seconds they were coursing towards the water at the bottom of the lower reservoir. They whirled and flurried through the air, Janey steering them ever onward towards Paulette, who had seen them approaching and was now trying to run faster, skidding on the chalky soil as she headed for the trees. 'I'm going down, Halo,' yelled Janey. 'You grab her!'

'OK!' Alfie's voice drifted up faintly from below. He was already aiming his legs towards Paulette.

By tipping her whole body forward, Janey managed to drive the sail down towards the path. She hung on as the whole kite shook like a leaf being torn from a branch, and Paulette looked up in terror as they descended on her.

'Gotcha!' Alfie scissored his ankles around Paulette's shoulders and let go of Janey's feet. 'Oof!'

Janey and the sail bounced up and forward again as Alfie's weight was released. Steering carefully, she veered around and came in to land.

'Ha! I wonder you can land on zose skinny little legs,' shouted Paulette.

Alfie had Paulette in a headlock on the gravel. She wasn't struggling, but lay instead sneering at Janey, a white handkerchief twitching in her hand. 'Surrender! Surrender, Alfie. So, Spylet wiz ze frozen brain, what are you going to do wiz me now?'

Alfie tightened his grip. 'We've got frozen brains, have we?'

'Oh, not you, Alfie, no!' protested Paulette,

gagging slightly as she tried to turn her head to look at him. 'No, just Janey 'ere.'

'Leave it, Al,' said Janey, taking the handkerchief from Paulette's hand. It was wet and rather slimy, but she could clearly see that it was actually two handkerchiefs sewn together . . . 'Where did you get this?'

'Maman gave it to me in case I caught a cold after running around near ze reservoir 'alf ze night,' said Paulette airily.

Janey stepped closer. 'That's Abe Rownigan's handkerchief. Where is he?'

Paulette shrugged. 'I don't know. Ze 'andkerchief was in ze water. Alfie, you are 'urting me.'

'That's sort of the point,' said Alfie.

'I can take you to ze place where I found it.'

'Good,' said Janey, and Alfie loosened his grip.

Paulette sat up slowly. 'It ees not so easy. You 'ave to give me somesing in return.'

Janey raised her eyebrows. Of course, she should have realized that no deal with an enemy could be that straightforward.

Paulette looked slyly from Janey to Alfie and back again. 'I will show you Rownigan, if you give me ze one sing I really, really want.'

'And what would that be?' asked Janey suspiciously.

A huge smile spread across Paulette's face as she took hold of the arm around her neck. ''Ave you not guessed, Spylet wiz a small brain? It is Alfie. To get Abe Rownigan, you 'ave to give me Alfie.'

Janey paled. Paulette had asked for something that was not hers to give. She shook her head, puzzled. 'I can't do that, Paulette. He's a person, not an old toy.'

'Quite right too, Blonde,' said Alfie angrily. 'Nobody's giving me away. Look, why are you so obsessed with me, Paulette?'

'I am not obsessed, Alfie. I love you, zat is all.'

Alfie flung his arm off Paulette as if he'd been electrocuted. 'Don't be an idiot,' he spluttered, looking as if he might vomit.

'I am not an idiot, Alfie,' said Paulette. 'It is natural zat I love you. After all, you are 'alf my brother.'

spy mums, spy dads

'Half your *what*?' gulped Janey, hoping desperately that she had misheard.

'My brother,' purred Paulette. 'Is zat not nice, Alfie? You have 'alf a sister zat you knew nussing about!'

Alfie shook his head as if he was waking himself from a nightmare. 'It's not true. I'm pretty sure Mum would have mentioned it if she'd had another baby.'

'*Non, non, non,* Alfie!' Paulette looked at him fondly. 'Your ugly mother wiz ze revolting teeth did not 'ave another baby. It ees your *father* who had another baby. Wiz his second wife – my beautiful Maman. And ze baby was *moi*!'

Janey watched the shock settle on to Alfie's face in a frozen mask and remembered instantly the confusion and pain she had experienced herself when she discovered that her Uncle Solomon was actually her father, Boz Brilliance Brown. 'Do you think it's possible, Al?' she said gently. 'Your dad didn't die, did he?'

'He . . . he just left, as far as I know.'

'And was he a diplomat like Paulette's father?'

Slowly Alfie nodded. 'Yes. And, well, a spy, of course. He went off to work in Europe – and sent postcards now and then.'

Janey suddenly realized something. Something terrible. 'Paulette, who is your father?' she asked solemnly.

'You must know by now! *C'est le Roi Soleil!* Ze Sun King, of course,' said Paulette, preening smugly. 'And 'e is *very* close by.'

'Why?' shouted Alfie. 'Why couldn't he just stay away?'

Paulette patted Alfie's hand. 'Our father wants very much to 'ave 'is family back, all around 'im. His spies, his wife, his daughter . . . and his son. You, Alfie.' Paulette gazed at her newfound sibling as if she'd been given all her Christmas presents at once. 'And once we force Solomon to change our rats back into people, we will learn the nine-lives secret – and we will be immortal! If you promise to leave Alfie wiz me, Janey, I will take you to zis Abraham Rownigan.'

Janey couldn't believe what she was hearing. 'It's up to Alfie what happens.'

The girl let out a peal of piercing laughter. 'Well, I am not so sure about that.' Paulette then pulled on the chain around her neck and produced a large locket. She opened it to reveal a double window. ''Ello, Papa, are you there? Per'aps you could show me who 'as come by today.'

The robotic answer chilled them. 'It's nice of your school to do home visits.'

Janey and Alfie watched, transfixed, as Paulette

147

showed them the image in her SPIV. From what appeared to be a black screen, the fuzzy picture sharpened. It was a tank, very deep and getting deeper as froth and foam gushed over the top. Pinned to the bottom was an anguished-looking Maisie Halliday. Her face bobbed like a balloon just above the surface scum of the rising water.

'Sorry, Alfie,' she said flatly. 'I had no idea what your father had been up to.'

'Mum!' shouted Alfie, but Paulette dropped the SPIV and the image disappeared. 'All right, I'll stay with you. As long as you take me straight to Mum, and help Janey find Abe.'

'You 'ave to come wiz me for always,' Paulette said in a sing-song voice. 'Or your mother will never get out from ze tank. You must promise, Alfie. You must say your goodbyes.'

'He can't promise that!' Janey yelled, outraged. 'That's so unfair!'

'And is it fair zat I should grow up wizout my brother? Is it fair zat my dear Maman has been turned into a RAT? And all because of you Browns. Alfie's mother, she got everysing, no? A good job, a nice 'ouse and my lovely Alfie. If we were rid of 'er we could all be together, and zen we would 'ave everysing. We are rich, true. But not rich in love.'

'You're completely nuts.' Alfie stood slowly, indicating to the path ahead of them. 'Bonkers. But I don't have a choice. I'll come with you to save my mum, but don't think it's for any other reason. You might be my sister, but nobody ever said you have to like your relatives.'

They didn't have a choice. Alfie's mum was in grave danger, and whichever fate befell her was too awful to contemplate – either a watery death or a life without her son. Janey knew what her own father would expect of her.

'You're sad, Paulette,' she said as they trudged past trees and bushes.

'Be quiet, Baguette-Legs,' Paulette snapped. 'Just remember, it is your fault. Zis 'ole sing. It is all your fault – you and zat uncle of yours. It is just lucky zat my papa was operating behind the scenes when Brown found out the team of scientists had discovered the nine-lives process. Your Solomon Brown changed my mother and her associates into rats. And you think it is *we* who are evil?'

'Save your energy, Blonde,' warned Alfie, so Janey silenced her retort. How she wished that her father was with her now. She couldn't help feeling that he had abandoned her. What help were his little messages when he wasn't able to follow up? Something, though, niggled away in the back of her mind. What had the last email said? 'Janey, to get to the point . . .'

As the realization hit her Janey caught her breath. Her father had sent someone to give her a SPI-buy, a gadget with a *point*! And there it was, pinned to her chest. She swallowed hard and unpinned her kite brooch quickly. She turned it over and looked hard. And there, under the pointed end of the pin, were the six little boxed numbers of the hallmark that Abe had shown her.

1   50   1   5   500   10

1, 50, 1, 5, 500, 10. Just ordinary numbers. Or were they? They were quite specific numbers, only ones, zeros, fives and tens. Her mind raced. What if she switched the numbers for *Roman* numerals?

OK, she thought to herself. Convert the number one – that's an I in Roman numerals. Now fifty – L. One again, so that's another I. Five's the letter V. Five hundred? Oh, not sure, not sure. Is it . . . D? Yes, I think it's D. And ten . . . ten is an X.'

Janey slowed down to keep the others at a distance and said the letters under her breath.

I   L   I   V   D   X

Suddenly she cracked the code. It *was* a message from her father. 'I live. Dad. Kiss.' 'Yes!' she said under her breath.

But she already knew that her dad was alive. She just didn't know where he was. At least she could now be sure that Abe Rownigan was friend, not foe. He'd been chosen by her father to pass a message to her – to hand over her badge of honour – and he had even drawn her attention to the hallmark. Abe must have been sent to protect Janey and her mother. And now she had possibly caused his death.

They had finally reached the far end of the lake. 'Where's my mum?' snarled Alfie.

'We go over ze motorway,' said Paulette.

Janey and Alfie both looked to where she was pointing. The Sun King beamed down at them from the banner above a set of grand gates.

'Of course. The Spylab,' said Janey.

Paulette laughed. 'Do you sink we would be so obvious? No. She is somewhere much more fun zan zat.'

the coach-doesn't-stop cafe

'Where. Is. My. Mother?' Alfie bounced on his Fleet-feet, ready to fly across the busy road to Sunny Jim's Swims.

'Al, we're in our SPIsuits!' hissed Janey. 'We can't just go running over there with all those people in the pool.'

'Ah! Twiglet 'as thought of somesing for once!'

'Enough of the name-calling, Paulette,' said Janey sharply. Her spy emotions buzzed through her – and one of them was pride. 'I might have skinny legs, but I've got a big heart. And at least I haven't got a *rat* for a mother. Now take us to Alfie's mum.'

Paulette crossed her arms sulkily. 'You 'ave not asked me nicely.'

It was as Janey had suspected. Paulette was just playing for time.

'No, I haven't, have I?' Grabbing Alfie's arm, Janey Fleet-footed across the road, leaving Paulette far behind in her ordinary trainers.

'No, wait! What if we don't find Mum in time? She'll drown! We need Paulette,' said Alfie. He looked back desperately at the French Spylet, who was pacing the gravel, waiting for a break in the traffic.

'You said it yourself, Halo – she's mad.' Janey bounded over the perimeter hedge and Alfie followed quickly. 'Besides, they have no honour, Al. Not like us. I tried to trade with them before, remember? She's not taking me to Abe Rownigan. She's not taking you to your mum. It's a trap!'

'Could be, Blonde. We can't expect all spies to act like us, even if –' he pretended to stick his fingers down his throat – 'euh, we're related to them. Well, what are we waiting for? Let's find my mum.'

'You check out the pools, I'll try the Coach-Stop Cafe. Come on!'

Paulette was now hopping around on the traffic island in the centre of the dual carriageway. Alfie took one last look at her and sped off to the pools, half-heartedly grabbing a towel to cover his SPIsuit legs. Janey hurried to the converted-coach cafe and opened the door.

'Not allowed here in swimsuits!' shouted the waitress who had shown Abe, Janey and her mum to their table just a few days ago. Janey smoothed her SPIsuit self-consciously.

'Sorry. Just needed some . . . water.'

The waitress blew out her cheeks. 'Just this once then. You don't look too wet. At the back near the kitchen.'

'Thanks.'

Janey scuttled past a couple of disinterested diners to

153

the little kitchen area next to the old driver's seat, but found nothing unusual at all.

She filled a glass with water so as not to arouse the waitress's suspicions and looked out of the front windscreen. Alfie was standing next to the showers with an extremely anguished expression, pointing to the floor. Behind him, a red-faced Paulette was advancing rapidly. Alfie hadn't seen her yet.

Janey was just about to run back down the coach and warn him when she noticed something. The big rear-view mirror of the coach showed the door at the back of the diner, and stepping through it was a tall, dark figure. Janey looked down. The shoes were long, thin and shiny black – the same shoes that had been about to touch down in the Sun King's Spylab the day she and Alfie had switched voices. And in place of his face the figure wore a sun-shaped mask that looked jagged and dangerous, like a drunken, evil star – the same star that had been drawn on the classroom window . . . The other diners just nodded and smiled, thinking he was someone dressed up as Sunny Jim from the water park. Only Janey knew the truth: it was the Sun King.

Alfie's mime had now become more agitated; he pointed to the shower cubicles and stretched himself up on his toes, poking his nose towards the sky. Mrs Halliday! He'd found where she was being held! Janey remembered the frothing white water pouring into the tank she was imprisoned in. It must be bubbling water from the showers, gushing down through the drain in the floor and flooding into the tank. From Alfie's desperate state, Janey guessed it was almost full. Paulette was now running into the shower block, turning on shower after shower, trying to hasten Mrs Halliday's end.

'Do something, Blonde. Now!' Janey said out loud. She looked again in the rear-view mirror. The Sun King was treading slowly, as if in pain. If he got much closer he would be able to overpower her and there might be nothing they could do to save Alfie's mum.

Janey had only one option. Hoping fervently that the Coach-Stop Cafe coach hadn't been completely gutted during its transformation into a diner, Janey leaped into the driver's seat.

Janey saw Alfie's eyes bulge behind his steamed-up Ultra-gogs as he registered what she was doing. It only took him a few moments to realize how he could help her out. He turned around so his back was to Janey, pretended to sit down and began an elaborate mime.

Janey copied his every move. 'OK, keys, turn. Come on, come on . . . yes!' After a tiny bit of coughing the old engine rumbled into life. 'Now, press foot down on left, shove the gearstick this way, foot down on right, come on!'

With a banshee's shriek the wheels of the old coach spun on the tarmac, as Janey pressed down on the accelerator and waggled the steering wheel. 'Argh! Why aren't we moving?'

She shrugged desperately at Alfie, who slapped his hand to his head and lunged into a mime again. 'Oh, this thing,' thought Janey, as she released the handbrake and pushed it down towards the floor.

Suddenly they were off, careering across the car park with motorists veering out of her way and families throwing themselves clear of the approaching coach. One family of diners was tipped off their booth on to the floor, rapidly followed by their burgers, cokes and a large order of coleslaw. Janey corrected the steering and the coach lurched over on to two wheels, every screw and bolt groaning. She watched in the mirror with delight as the Sun King grabbed the juke box, bringing it down on top of him. He was trapped.

Alfie was now occupied with fighting Paulette. They both turned as Janey blasted the horn, signalling to Alfie to get out of the way. Just in time, he flung himself over the grass verge towards the lockers, but not before Paulette had managed to free herself from his grasp and run out of sight. Janey wrenched the wheel around ninety degrees and headed straight for the shower cubicles.

Her aim had to be precise, but as she got closer and closer she began to worry that she'd made a huge mistake. How could one old coach smash down a whole shower block?

Janey braced herself as the coach hit the corner of the showers with an ear-grinding crunch. Janey was thrown back against the driver's seat and would have ricocheted forward into the steering wheel if she hadn't reached over her head and gripped the back of the seat with her Girl-gauntlet.

As the coach slammed into it, the shower block tipped like a felled tree. The metal sides buckled and swayed, and with every inch the coach moved forward the walls dipped further towards the ground. Soap dispensers and drying equipment were wrenched from the walls and sent spinning across Sunny Jim's Swims as the shower block creaked an anguished, final death rattle and fell, shattered, to the ground.

Janey almost fell out of the driver's door in her eagerness to find Mrs Halliday. Alfie ran to meet her at the centre of the destroyed shower room, a large square that covered the main drain.

'She's under there!' Janey fished her SPIder out of her SPIsuit and thrust it through the grating. 'Try and grab that, Mrs H! Breathe, while we get you out!'

Alfie leaped on to the grille, curled his Boy-battler and pummelled the rivets holding it in place as if he was wielding a mallet. In just a few moments several of the screws had come loose, but even between them the two Spylets did not have enough power to lift the grille more than a couple of centimetres.

'It's hopeless!' screamed Alfie.

'No! Loosen the other corner.' Janey waited while Alfie set to work again. 'Good. Now, slide your ASPIC through the gap – it'll work, Al, honestly. OK, stand on the grille directly over your ASPIC. I'll do it too.' Janey felt the magnetic force clamping the ASPIC to her Fleet-feet. 'When I say jump, jump. One, two, three . . . JUMP!'

With every bit of strength they had, the Spylets both hoisted one foot up through the air, away from the magnetic pull of the ASPIC. Sweat streamed down their faces and Janey felt as though her neck would burst open with the effort. She waved a hand at Alfie and they allowed their Fleet-feet to bash back down against the grille. Their feet exploded in unison. The grille was ripped upwards like the lid of a tin can, then thrown back to the ground a metre or so away, with Janey and Alfie still attached to it.

Rubbing their ankles, they released themselves and ran back over to the drain. Mrs Halliday had water and soap suds flipping in little waves over her head, but she was chewing furiously. The SPIder had saved her. She bobbed up to the surface and smiled gratefully. 'Thank you, Spylets.'

Alfie held out his hand to help his mother clamber out. 'Some things you'd like to tell me?' he said brusquely.

Maisie Halliday nodded slowly, ruffling her son's hair. 'I think so, Al.'

Janey stepped back. This was a private moment. She knew only too well what it felt like to have your father's unexpected past brought home to you. She only wished she knew where her own dad was right now. She gave her kite badge a little stroke. 'I live too . . . Dad. Find me soon.' She pictured the familiar face that she saw every night when she secretly conjured his image from the LipSPICK – the way he leaned over Trouble, stroking his head and saying . . . 'what I've created . . . what I've created . . .'

And right then Jane Blonde realized something huge. Her heart sank so far it felt as though it was thrashing around in her stomach. She *had* let the cat out of the bag, just as the Sun King said. That was why he was so convinced that Trouble used to be a frog. He'd seen it. He'd seen Trouble. He'd seen Solomon. He'd watched the LipSPICK recording.

Janey's throat went dry. She had betrayed her father. No. It was even worse than that. By watching the LipSPICK, even though she knew it was forbidden, Janey had betrayed them all.

spi let-down

G-Mamma couldn't even look at her pupil and god-daughter. Mascara had run down her face and across her blushered cheeks in thick black streaks, and she trembled from head to foot. Whether it was with despair, or rage – or both – Janey didn't know.

She tried again. 'G-Mamma, you have to understand what it was like. I'd never met him. I didn't even know my father was alive. I wasn't going to keep the bit of LipSPICK, I mean, I didn't set out to steal it. It was just there, on my finger, and it was just like a photo really. I didn't think it would cause any harm . . .'

'But it wasn't just a photo, was it? It was *evidence*.' G-Mamma sighed. 'And the harm you've done is . . . well, I can't even bear to think about it.'

Neither could Janey. She'd unleashed chaos. She'd even let someone – the Sun King – see the identity of the head of Solomon's Polificational Investigations after that information had been hidden for at least a decade. The enemy knew that Boz was still alive. Janey had a hand in destroying him – and maybe all the other spies in Solomon's

Polificational Investigations. And she might have allowed power-crazed villains the world over to do whatever they wanted, because there would be nobody – no SPI organization, no Boz Brown – to stop them. Tears rolled down Janey's face.

'You'd better de-Wow, Janey,' said G-Mamma quietly, 'and hand over your badge.'

'But . . .' Janey grasped the little kite that Abe Rownigan had given her. 'What do you mean, hand it over?'

G-Mamma thought for a few moments, pursing her rosy lips. 'All right. You can keep the badge – I suppose that was a gift as much as anything else. You can hang on to that, and to your other SPI-buys. They won't mean anything more to you once you've been brain-wiped. Don't worry,' she added in a quavering whisper, 'there'll be no painful memories. No memories . . . at all.'

'But . . . you can't do that to me!' Janey could hardly breathe. 'G-Mamma, please. I understand that what I did was terribly, terribly bad and silly and selfish and a million other things, but you can't take away all my memories of . . . all this. My dad . . . you . . .'

Her godmother was sobbing openly now with great heaving breaths. 'Janey, Janey, Janey. Haven't I always told you that trust is everything? You deceived me, us, all of us. You betrayed your father. There's no going back from that.'

'No!' screamed Janey. 'You can't do that! You mustn't! I'm the daughter of Boz Brilliance Brown.

He told me in front of you that *I'm* his spy now. I'm the one he trusts!'

G-Mamma got to her feet. 'How can he trust you now? You acted as a *daughter*, and not as a spy. That will never do.'

Janey sank on to the stool. 'Oh, what have I done?'

G-Mamma simply shrugged. Even Trouble, sitting behind the mirror on the SPI:KE's make-up counter, was managing to look Janey up and down in a way that suggested he was hugely disappointed in her.

'I'm so, so sorry.'

'Janey,' said G-Mamma seriously, 'for once in my life I don't know what else to say. I may never rap again. Let's just . . . get this over with.'

Janey stood up as slowly as possible. She could understand what it would have been like for the aristocrats in the French revolution, on the way to the guillotine. She was walking to her death: the death of one half of her, of Jane Blonde, Sensational Spylet.

G-Mamma hovered behind her as she edged towards the Wower. Once she was in there, her Lycra SPIsuit would be replaced by ordinary civilian clothes; her Ultra-gogs would disappear; her hair would return to pale, insignificant brown. Like Janey herself. Pale, insignificant Brown. No friends, no life, no father.

But just as G-Mamma reached across to pull open the Wower door, Janey realized something. Her SPI:KE was wrong. She had said that to be a Spylet, Janey could never act as a daughter, only as a spy. But hadn't her father acted as a *dad* as well as a spy? Hadn't he insisted that she be trained up as a Spylet because the bonds that held them together were greater than those of even the most loyal and treasured SPI employee? Come to think of it, wasn't she a Spylet precisely *because* she was the daughter of Boz Brilliance Brown and the one-time superSPI Gina Bellarina?

Janey's breath quickened. G-Mamma was snivelling loudly and dabbing at her panda eyes with the edge of her chiffon wrap. Janey knew she had to do something, right now. Zippety split, as G-Mamma would say.

She steeled herself as her SPI:KE stood to one side of the Wower to let her in. 'G-Mamma,' Janey began, 'I'll never see you again. And even if I do, I won't remember who you are. Could you let me keep your lovely scarf? It's so . . . you.' Nodding blearily, G-Mamma handed over the chiffon wrap. Janey hesitated. 'And . . . and one last hug?'

G-Mamma howled balefully and reached out her arms to clap Janey to her quivering chest. It was now or never. Janey felt a surge of power course through her as she grabbed G-Mamma's hands and kissed them. Then, with a sorrowful, 'I'm sure you'll understand!' she shoved her godmother backwards into the Wower.

Janey slammed the door home with her foot, then speedily looped the chiffon scarf through the handles and tied a tight knot. G-Mamma hollered from inside the Wower cubicle but then turned her attention to fighting off the robotic hands that were reaching for her from all angles of the Wower. 'Get your nasty little metal fingers . . . ow! What are you doing! That's designer! Leave me alone, I don't want Wowing!'

Janey turned to Trouble, who was watching her warily from the counter. 'Don't think badly of me, Trubs. I know what I have to do. I have to find my dad.' Grabbing all the messages that Sol had sent to her over the last few days, Janey held the ASPIC above her head and ran for the window. 'Let her out in ten minutes – your sabre-claw thing will go through the chiffon in no time. I'll be back when my mission is completed. Goodbye!'

And with that, Jane Blonde launched herself out through the window and down the wall, across G-Mamma's front lawn and over the top of the approaching Clean Jean van, then over the road and into the fields.

brown again

Janey reached the reservoir and clambered into Abe Rownigan's Daimler. While there was a chance he was still alive Janey had to try to find him – he might be able to lead her to her dad, and anyway she wanted to say sorry. But how? The message she had received from her father about the 'new guy' had said, 'You can say that again.' What did it mean?

'New guy, new guy, new guy,' said Janey over and over, until the words ran together and she hardly knew whether 'guy' came before 'new' or the other way round. 'New guy, new guy. Oh, it doesn't make sense. What if I say his actual name? Rownigan, Rownigan, Rownigan . . .'

It was getting her nowhere, so Janey looked again at the email her dad had sent.

. . . that type of thing is BIG . . . Afraid can't help. Busy right now. End of special project. In touch soon. Stay well, UNCLE SOLOMON

Maybe it wasn't a straightforward rejection after all. But what was the code? With a tiny firework explosion in Janey's head, she knew the answer and the actual message leaped off the page at her.

'You idiot, Blonde! He's asking for me to look for the BIG type – at the capital letters. A for afraid, B for busy, E . . . I . . . S . . . ABE IS. Abe is! But Abe is what? No, it can't be! UNCLE SOLOMON is in capitals too. So . . .' Her eyes widened as she read the message aloud. 'Abe is Uncle Solomon.'

Janey hooted with joy. She'd found her dad. It was Abe! Suddenly everything made sense. 'No wonder he loves Mum! I was so horrid to him!' Her mood sobered. 'He was trying to rescue me. That night at the dam, he came because I said I needed help. And he . . . he went right over the edge.'

Janey already felt as if her insides were trying to escape. 'I might have killed my own father.'

But Abe Rownigan looked so different to her dad. Much taller, different hair, brown eyes. So unless he's had a very extreme makeover, there had to be another explanation. Janey's jaw dropped. Could the Crystal Clarification Process have been used on a human? Had her father used it on *himself*?'

It was almost too much to take in at once, but Janey knew one thing for sure. Her father was still her father, whatever he looked like. And she had to find him. Now.

Janey was so filled with panic that she hardly noticed the hissing sound in the car getting louder. It had now increased to a hum, and with a start Janey noticed that it wasn't coming from the car at all. She jumped out. It was

coming from *underneath* the car – from the SPI-Pod that
G-Mamma had planted! More voices were filtering
through the humming background noise. 'It would be
much easier if you just showed us 'ow you do ze brain
swap.'

'Yes, come along, Mr Rownigan,' rasped the Sun
King. 'Then we can let you go and we'll do it ourselves.'

'Only I can perform the procedure,' said Abe firmly.

Janey's heart stopped at the sound of her father's
voice.

He continued, 'Solomon Brown trusted me, and me
alone, to carry out the surgery. The brain replacement is a
highly complex operation.'

He was stalling for time by pretending he knew all
about the brain swap that Janey had completely invented.

'Start the refreezing process on the water rats,' Abe
said, 'and tell me where your store of human brains is so I
can prepare them properly.'

Suddenly the dull robotic drone cut in. 'The rats and
their new brains are being united at this very moment.
Five human brains. Pity they are all. So. Small!'

Janey's blood ran cold as these words sank in, and she
got urgently to her feet by the Daimler. 'G-Mamma!'
she said urgently into her SPIV. 'Are you still trapped in
the Wower?'

The SPIV crackled as G-Mamma's pale, stretched
face loomed into view. The SPI:KE was bobbing her
head to and fro, humming nervously. 'Ummm,
noooo. Little rap for you though . . . Nothing can

be said, cos we're all in the shed, like the poor little cat, we're surrounded by rats. Ow! Get off!' Janey heard some scrabbling around in the background and then deadly silence as G-Mamma dropped her SPIV and lost contact.

Five human brains. Janey knew without a doubt who the five would be: G-Mamma, Maisie Halliday, Alfie, her mother . . . and Janey herself when she went to rescue them. The Sun King believed in Janey's made-up brain-swap procedure so fully that the brains of her own nearest and dearest were about to be transplanted into the five water rats. What should she do?

'. . . release them,' Abe Rownigan was saying slowly. 'Jane Blonde was lying. There is no brain-swap procedure. I'll tell you the proper way to turn the rats back into humans if you let those people go.'

'No!' screamed Janey. Surely her dad wasn't really going to give up his precious secret . . .

She had to get to him first. He was still the Sun King's most valuable hostage. If they had him, they had the secret. Without him, they were nothing. But where was he?

She leaned in closer to the SPI-Pod. 'Come on,' she whispered. 'Give me a clue.' Paulette was now trying to persuade Abe Rownigan and Solomon Brown to come back on the team with Copernicus, the former government official who had turned bad and already tried once to destroy SPI. So Copernicus had masterminded this mission as well . . .

'Solomon Brown will never trust Copernicus again, Paulette,' said Abe. 'That's just not an option.'

'But you can make up your own mind, yes? No, Claude, not now please!'

Claude, mouthed Janey. Who on earth was Claude? Ha! Alfie had got it wrong. It wasn't *Clod* the Cook. It was *Claude,* the French chef. Abe was at Paulette's house!

It was just along the Quarry Road, so Janey took to her Fleet-feet and sprinted up the chalk-and-gravel driveway until it widened into a tarmac road. The black surface flew beneath her feet as she sped towards the high hedge in front of Paulette's house.

Instinctively Janey knew where Abe was being held, and she crept through the bushes to the swimming pool. Just left of the pool was a crane holding a concrete disk a couple of metres above the ground. The bowed black outline of a man blocked Janey's view of the water, but she could make out Paulette on the other side, dangling her petite feet in the water as if she was enjoying a day out. Every so often she would kick out with a dainty toe and watch the water arcing up into the air.

'Stop that, Paulette,' barked the man, the Sun King. He loomed over his daughter. 'Concentrate on the job in hand.'

The starlit surface of the pool was so milky with light that Janey found it hard to make things out. What she could see, however, brought a lump to her throat.

Abe Rownigan. Solomon Brown. Boz 'Brilliance' Brown. Her dad was stretched like a starfish across the surface of the pool, with ropes attached to his wrists and ankles. Only his face was visible above the waterline.

'Well, Abe Rownigan,' said the Sun King, leaning over the pool, 'we will continue the reversal process that the imbecile Jane Blonde told us. Perhaps you have been double-bluffing. Never bluff a bluffer, I say. You have been stalling us, but have you run out of time? Perhaps we need to . . . let's say . . . *persuade* Jane Blonde to tell us more.'

'No! I'll tell you,' shouted Abe, 'if you let Solomon's family and friends go.'

Paulette put a finger on her chin, as if she was considering it carefully. 'Er, *non*. We sink *you* are ze one making sings up. You do not know anysing at all. And Papa is getting impatient, aren't you, Papa? Even if it means killing 'is own lovely son, we will find out from Jane Blonde. So I sink it is time we say bye-bye Monsieur Rownigan.'

Two things hit Janey at once. The first was her dad's fake name. Of course! 'You can say that again,' his first email had said. Abe Rownigan. Abe Rownigan. Aberownigan. Abrownigan. A Brown again! The clues had been there right from the outset.

The second was far more sinister. The Sun King had moved away from Paulette and was making his way slowly over to the crane. Janey looked up at the concrete disk dangling from it, her heart sinking. The disk was extremely thick, impenetrable and looked to be the exact diameter of the pool. When it descended it would be like putting a very tight plug in a plughole. And trapped underneath it would be her father.

She had to move. Perhaps she could overpower the Sun King. Tiptoeing as close as she dared, Janey looked around for something to fight with, just as the Sun King clambered into the driver's seat and started pushing levers.

And Janey could not stop herself from running out of the bushes and shouting out, 'No!'

spies and spiders

The concrete plug swung towards Janey. She backed away from the zigzagging crane but it tracked her every move.

'Finally ze small brain works!' said Paulette, watching with delight from the other side of the pool.

'How can you be related to Alfie? You're evil!' shouted Janey furiously, skidding out of the way.

'Ah yes, well, zat is sad. I did not expect him to be so . . . good! But 'e 'as not 'ad our father's influence.'

'Janey, just run,' shouted Abe Rownigan from the pool. 'They won't catch you!'

'I'm not going without you!' cried Janey.

'How right you are,' said the Sun King, surging forward with the crane. 'We can just take your brain right now.'

He swung the rock pendant at her, and as Janey stepped backwards to avoid it she plummeted straight into the pool. Through her Ultra-gogs, she saw a golden shape embossed on the bottom of the pool, its points reaching up the sides. It was a sun. If only Alfie had noticed it when he first came round for a swim. She surfaced quickly and swam to Abe, where she pulled desperately at a rope attached to his wrist. 'Come on, we've got to get out.'

'Get yourself out, Janey,' he said. 'There isn't time to untie me.'

'No!' Janey's fingers scrabbled at the ties, but the wet rope slithered through her grip. Finally she managed to untie the first wrist, but it was too late. The concrete plug was being lowered towards them. It skimmed the edge of the pool with a harsh grating sound as the Sun King guided it over the hole, and then the light disappeared as the disk sank into position.

Janey was forced under the water. Abe Rownigan, too, was pushed below the surface, still tied to the pool edge by ropes that were now trapped beneath several tons of impenetrable concrete. Janey felt for her SPIder, wishing desperately that she had thought to bring a spare. Abe's eyes were closing, even as he turned his head to try to see what Janey was doing.

Her long-lost father, so recently found again, was drifting away before her very eyes. The SPIder filled her lungs with oxygen and Janey swam to her father's ankles, pointing her Girl-gauntlet at the rope. But the laser finger seemed useless underwater. Her father's head had lolled right back in the water and his mouth was open, water glugging straight into his lungs.

She swam round to lift up his head. If only there was some way to share the SPIder . . .

Before it was too late, Janey sucked in a big

gulp of oxygen, pulled the rubbery gum from her mouth and slid it between her father's lips. A split second later, her father's eyes opened. Janey pulled off her Girl-gauntlet and bit the end of the little finger. Her teeth ripped through the material and she flinched at the acrid taste. Stun-gas. She squeezed the glove, forcing all the gas into the water, where it dispersed harmlessly. Then, with a quick prayer, Janey put the glove over her father's mouth like an oxygen mask, slid the little finger into her own mouth and breathed.

At first only water slipped between her lips. It wasn't working. She tried again, and this time felt a bubble of air pop into her mouth. Janey drew in a deep breath and felt a rush of exhilaration and relief as oxygen flooded into her lungs at the same time as her father looked at her with wide eyes, alert and surprised.

Janey gave him a thumbs-up, and he returned it with his free hand. The water had made the ropes that tied him heavy, so Janey pulled out the pen nib from the index finger of her ruined Girl-gauntlet. The tiny blade glinted in her hand as she began to saw through the fibres. After a few minutes Abe was free, and the two of them bobbed about with their hair brushing against the underside of the concrete plug, still sharing the SPIder.

Janey's mind raced. How were they going to get out? Her mother and her dearest friends needed her to rescue them, but the concrete plug had them completely trapped. Janey looked helplessly at her dad. She could see now that when he smiled his eyes, though brown instead of blue, crinkled in exactly the same way as she remembered.

But how come his eyes were above the water?

Janey glanced down. The water was now below her nose. Cautiously, she spat the gauntlet finger from her mouth as her father removed the glove from his face.

He passed the SPIder to Janey. 'Thank you. You saved my life – again.'

'I put you in danger, you mean. I'm sorry, D-Dad.'

'No, you didn't,' he said gently.

'I did! I held back a bit of LipSPICK, I'm so sorry. I played it every night on my ceiling because I missed you so much. The Sun King must have seen it. He must have been spying on me . . .'

'So that's how he knew I was still alive! It's a good job I had changed my appearance so radically. I'd heard that someone calling himself the Sun King was a threat, so after I'd dealt with the Sinerlesse I went to track him down, but he was being protected by five of his top agents. When some intelligence told me that the Sun King's spies had discovered the secret to a cat's nine lives, I knew they were just too dangerous. I couldn't allow that secret to escape. The Sun King insisted that he be the first to undergo the procedure. He had become obsessed with the idea of immortality. But the procedure went wrong and his face and throat were horribly damaged. That's why he wears that sun mask and uses a voice changer. And he needs water around him always, as he needs regular bathing to stop the burning.

Anyway, his spies managed to refine the process by the time I could break into their lab, so I had no choice. I Crystal-Clarified them into rats, then left you that message on the window at school.'

'Scat cat, rat pack. I knew it meant that Trouble was in . . . well, Trouble. But aren't you angry with me about the LipSPICK?'

Abe smiled. 'Do you know the other reason I changed my appearance and kept it a secret? I hoped it would be a way for us to be together again, as a family,' he said, hugging Janey to him. 'Of course I understand. You weren't thinking, you were feeling. Like me trying to bring us all back together again. I didn't think it through very well.'

'No, it would have been brilliant. It still can be! But I knew you were still alive somewhere. I couldn't let Mum be with someone else.'

Her father's eyes crumpled at the corners. 'I underestimated your loyalty to me, Janey.'

The water level was now halfway down the pool wall, and Janey could see the great golden sun just a metre or so beneath their feet. They were treading water easily.

'The pool's draining out. We'll be able to stand on the bottom soon,' said Abe, reaching out a long leg. 'Then we can work out a way to get out of here.'

But Janey knew that something wasn't right. Beneath their feet, the prongs of the golden sun were twisting, and the floor of the pool was opening. The rays of the golden sun separated, rising up through the water with edges that were rapier sharp. Janey and Abe were forced back into the middle of the pool with water squelching and swirling away through the spikes under their feet. As the water started to spin like a whirlpool Janey reached out for her dad's hand. The sun opened up like a chrysanthemum, and they hovered for one brief, dark moment over a black, bottomless chute . . .

The water plummeted, slapping against the sides of the enormous drainpipe. Janey screamed, grappling to hang on to her father's hand as they were sucked down the chute, twisting and tumbling through the dank, fetid air. As they fell Janey heard a loud crack in the distance. The water beneath them had made contact with the bottom of the drain. To Janey's horror, the noise was followed by a gurgle as the water drained away. They were now free-falling on to bare stone.

Janey felt faint with dread. No sooner had she found her father again than they were both about to be dashed against the drain floor like ice cubes in the bottom of a glass. This wasn't like the Spylab entry cylinder, where a steadying cushion of air softened the landing. It was hopeless. Or . . . was it?

With not a moment to spare, Janey ripped the SPIder from her pocket and shoved it into her mouth. She chomped furiously.

The gum was loose and flexible in her mouth. Janey forced a tiny bit through her lips as they somersaulted down the tunnel like a pair of trapeze artists. Janey could blow ordinary gum into a bubble the size of her head, and she knew this was no ordinary gum. This was SPI-gum. She chewed and blew harder. She could see the ground fast approaching – they had only seconds. But the bubble was massive now and shimmered below them like an airbed. Just as the floor rose up to greet them, Janey twisted the bubble and spat it out of her mouth. It drifted to the ground, and she and her father fell on to it with an almighty smack.

It broke their fall like a safety mattress. They catapulted off it against the slimy sides of the tunnel and bounced up and down until they finally came to a stop.

'Amazing!' said Janey. A protective bubble like this could save your life, again – and again – and again.

'Good work, Blonde,' said Abe. 'However did you think of that?'

Janey grinned. 'I'm just really good at blowing bubbles.' But something was nagging away at her. She just couldn't put her finger on what.

Abe jumped off the SPIder mattress as it deflated rapidly. 'Well, these poor devils obviously didn't have such good luck.' He extracted a broken bone that had punctured the bubble and pointed with it to a pair of skeletons entangled on the rock floor.

Janey shuddered. 'Come on! We've got to stop the Sun King.'

sinking the sun king

After climbing out of a manhole a little further along Quarry Road, Janey Fleet-footed to the reservoir with her father in her slipstream, sliding along on the ASPIC. They got into the Daimler. 'Everyone's trapped in the garden shed,' she said quickly. 'That's where the Sun King is headed. He'll kill them.' They had just seen how ruthless he could be.

Abe flung the car into gear and screeched out of the reservoir car park. 'Janey, do you know why the Sun King thinks he's so important?'

'Because he's mad?'

Abe laughed. 'Well, yes, but also because the sun is the centre around which the other planets rotate.'

'So he thinks he's the centre of the universe.'

'Exactly. But who was the first person to discover that the other planets moved around the sun, and not around the Earth?'

Janey shook her head. How could this be important at a time like this?

'The name of that astronomer, Janey,' said Abe with a sigh, 'was Copernicus.'

'Copernicus?' Janey spluttered. 'So are you saying that you think the Sun King is actually Copernicus himself?'

Abe nodded grimly.

'So if the Sun King is actually Copernicus, that means . . . Oh blimey. Alfie's dad is Copernicus! He is not going to like that.'

At that moment they pulled up outside Janey's house, dashed out of the car and raced through the garden. Janey flung open the door to the shed with a warrior-cry. 'Oh,' she squeaked. 'There's nobody here.'

The shed was completely undisturbed. Not even the cobwebs had been moved. 'But G-Mamma said they were all in the shed, with poor Trouble. Or maybe she said *like* poor Trouble.' She racked her brains. 'I've got the wrong shed! She meant the shed that Trouble got caught in – your car-wash building!'

They sprinted back to the car. 'You can't fool animals, Janey,' said Abe. 'Trouble has known all along who I am. He was trying to reach me that night.'

'That's why he ran to the car wash! And climbed up your leg . . .'

'So you're sure that's where they'll be now?'

Janey nodded swiftly. 'Hurry, Dad!'

Her father slammed his foot on the accelerator and they sped to Abe 'n' Jean's Clean Machines. Minutes later, they screeched to a halt outside the car wash.

'You'd put the signs up already.' Janey looked sadly at the banners declaring that A & J's would be open that day.

A couple of cars were already lined up on the road outside, badly in need of a clean.

Her father shrugged. 'I really wanted to make a go of it, Janey. It could have been the making of us.'

'Instead of the death of us. Come on.'

Janey got out of the car and strode towards the car wash, with her father close behind her. She peered through the clear plastic doors. Jean Brown was standing with her arms folded, looking annoyed and anxious at the same time, while the Halos and G-Mamma stood warily, back to back, with Trouble in the little space between their legs. Surrounding the group were five snarling water rats, guarding the entrance and exit to the car wash and snapping at anyone who dared move.

'Listen here,' said Janey's mother, 'give me my daughter back, and you can have the business. That's what your little message meant, isn't it? The picture of Janey attached to the photograph of this place. Is that why we're all here? Just give me back my daughter!'

Abe winced. 'We'd better get in there. Ready?'

'Not in my lifetime,' said a demonic, robotic voice behind them. 'Not in any of my lifetimes!'

Janey and Abe span around. The Sun King, Copernicus himself, was poised over the controls of an enormous ambulance, his expression hidden as ever by the glinting golden mask. Paulette sat beside him, cooly inspecting her fingernails.

'Be my guest,' said Abe, waving an arm at the

car wash. 'If you flatten the place, you'll kill the water rats, and that will make my life so much easier.'

Copernicus laughed evilly. 'No, that is not so. If we flatten the place, the water rats will survive. It is only the sad humans who would be squashed.'

'You don't want to do that,' yelled Janey. 'You want their brains! That's why you've brought an ambulance with you!'

'How true. Your brain must be bigger than I thought. And you escaped the Death Drop in my pool too! Fine. We'll take your brain first.'

The great white vehicle advanced towards them. They were trapped between its advancing wheels and the closed door to the car wash. In one way or another, Janey owed her life to every one of the people trapped within the car-wash shed and the man standing beside her now, ready and willing to fight, but all out of options. Through the ambulance's windscreen Janey saw Copernicus lean forward as he stepped on the accelerator.

Janey thought back to her first visit to the car wash. It seemed like a century ago that she had stood and watched a grimy car appear so stunningly transformed before them. It was a very special car wash . . .

Out of the side of her mouth, Janey hissed to Abe Rownigan, 'Is there a reason that cars come out of here looking *so* good?'

Abe's eyes fixed on the monster rolling relentlessly towards them. 'You've read my mind, Blonde! The button's down to your left.'

They couldn't afford to wait a second longer. Janey reached out a hand to the sparkling silver button on her left and yelled at the top of her voice:

'Prepare to be Wowed, everybody! One, two, THREE!'

She slammed her fist on the button and the car wash, the biggest Wower known to SPI-dom, burst into action. As jets of water glistened around the people and creatures in the shed, Janey ran straight forward and wedged her ASPIC under the front wheel of the ambulance. Even bearing such a huge weight, the hoverboard lifted off the ground so that the wheels spun aimlessly. The engine whined like a drill as Copernicus threw the gearstick around, trying but failing to get any traction.

'That won't stop me, you foolish little girl,' he crowed. 'I am the centre of the universe!'

Abe Rownigan had moved around to the power hose on the far side of the shed. Janey took a step backwards, gathered herself together and then ran like a demon. Straight up the bonnet of the ambulance she went, over Copernicus and Paulette, then over the roof in a neat Fleet-feet flip. She pounded across to a second power hose as both evil spies opened their doors. Janey had no need to signal to her father what he should do. He was already opening the hose, pointing it directly into the driver's cabin.

'It won't hold them long, Blonde,' he shouted, 'but it will buy us some time.'

Janey picked up her own power hose, and at exactly the same moment they each opened a nozzle to full throttle. Water cannoned at Copernicus and Paulette from either side and they crashed heads as the full force smashed into them. They clung to each other miserably, being tossed around in the cabin as if they were sitting in a whale's spout.

Suddenly the doors to the car wash opened behind them. Janey turned around and almost dropped the hose in astonishment. Four humans and a cat had been through the car-wash Wower. She was used to seeing Trouble with his quiff and Al Halo in his denim boiler suit, but the others were transformed. G-Mamma was resplendent in a fuchsia-pink trouser suit, with a gold-loop SuSPInder hooked casually around her waist and large fluorescent Ultra-gogs beneath a rippling orange headscarf. A similar suit in olive green with military buttons fitted Mrs Halliday perfectly, and poised next to Trouble was Gina Bellarina, SuperSPI.

'Wow,' said Janey and her father in unison.

Jean Brown was completely transformed. Her short brown hair now clung to her skull in the sharpest of burnished gold bobs. Enhanced by wing-framed Ultra-gogs, her eyes glowed with hazel fire, and from head to toe she was encapsulated in a shimmering bronze SPIsuit. To Janey, standing open-mouthed with a gushing water cannon in her hand, her mother looked like the statuette given out at the Oscars.

The Wower had not, however, been able restore all Gina's spy memories and skills, so the old Jean Brown was still in charge of the new image.

'Janey, you're here! What are you doing? And Abe, you're back!?'

'Sorry, Jean, no time for fond little catch-ups,' roared G-Mamma, whipping around like a deep-pink cyclone. 'Water rats incoming! Furry formations at one-eighty degrees!'

'Trouble, sit on this hose!' Janey waited until the cat was in position, training the water jet on Paulette and Copernicus, then ran to join her SPI unit at the doorway to the car-wash shed. She gulped. 'Oh. My. Word.'

The rats had been Wowed too – and it was so diabolical that Janey could hardly bear to look.

spy-cats, rat-dogs

'It's a m-m-monster!'

As it did to everyone that passed beneath its sprays of technological brilliance, the Wower had taken the best features of the rats and enhanced them. And the best feature of the water rats was the fact that they were completely loyal, sticking to each other through good times and bad like stinking, noxious glue.

The creature prowling the floor of the car wash, drooling saliva from its blood-red jaws, appeared at first glance to be a ferocious tan-coloured Dobermann. But it was actually five different entities, one forming each leg, the fifth straddling the others to make up the body and head. Around the whole nightmarish creature was a caul, oozing with slime and gore as it encased the water-rat-beast in a kind of glistening bubble.

Alfie charged forward, Boy-battler poised. As his fist pummelled the foul creature the head snapped and slavered at him; Alfie's hand bounced back off the surface of the bubble and flew back into his face. 'Agh!' He slumped to the floor.

The bubble's protecting it, thought Janey.

'Al!' Mrs Halliday sprang forward and dragged her son out of harm's way as quickly as possible. Janey squeezed the middle finger of her ripped Girl-gauntlet. A shaft of intense light shot into the creature's eyes and it howled with pain before knocking her out of the way.

G-Mamma body-rolled to Janey's flank, pushed her sideways and then continued to crawl beneath the belly of the beast, avoiding the five snapping faces. She whipped off her gold-chain SuSPInder and threw it over the creature's back, trying to lasso it from underneath. It reared up, tossing its head to and fro in rage and ripping the chain from her hand. 'Bad beastie!' she shouted. 'Sit!'

The creature was now making for the doorway. Mrs Halliday attempted a swipe at it, catching the beast a glancing blow on its back, but her hand simply ricocheted off the protective bubble and she was propelled back with a great force. Suddenly, Gina Bellarina was left alone in the doorway to face the hideous enemy.

'Jean, look out!' Abe Rownigan and Alfie were now tying Paulette and Copernicus up with one of the hosepipes, face down on the gravelled track of the car wash. The scarlet angry skin on the back of Copernicus's neck glistened beneath the edge of his mask.

The monstrous rat-beast slavered savagely. 'Look out, it's after you, Mum!' shouted Janey, racing towards her mother.

'Oh, is it now?' said Gina Bellarina sternly. 'Well, I've had quite enough of being attacked in my own house –' she karate-chopped the creature's skull – 'and my own business –' she kick-boxed the beast in the chest – 'and alongside my own friends and family.' As a finale, she leaped up in the air and drop-kicked her dazed opponent.

Janey wanted to cheer at the magnificence of Gina Bellarina, but as she reached her mother and turned around she knew that it was too soon to celebrate. The beast was back on its feet, moving relentlessly towards the source of its irritation and focus, who was sitting obediently on a hosepipe, lapping occasionally at the sprays of water that spurted past him.

'It's after Trouble! Run!' Janey raced towards her Spycat and shoved him out of the beast's way. Trouble was thrown up in the air but managed to rotate, land on his feet and take off around the shed like the hare on a greyhound track, his go-faster stripes a blur and his quiff streaming straight out behind him like a flag.

The rat-beast lifted its head to the pink afternoon sky and yowled menacingly, then coiled its muscles. It took off after Trouble, lurching grotesquely as the five creatures coordinated their vile slinking movements into one.

Suddenly the evil robot voice of Copernicus coughed into life. 'Ding dong bell, pussy's in the well.' He barked his horrible rasp of a laugh as one hand snaked out of the coil of hosepipe in which he was imprisoned and pointed the nozzle at Trouble's retreating back. He was trying to train the few drips of water still coming from the hose on to her cat.

And suddenly Janey got it.

'Dad, G-Mamma, that's why they kept Trouble in that tank while they were doing experiments on him! That glimmering skin-thing the rat-beast is covered in – it's like the SPIder bubble we landed on at the bottom of the Death Drop. I think that's why cats have nine lives – they've got a natural protective bubble around them! That must be why all the pictures of Trouble at the Sun King's Spylab were shiny. His bubble was working. But think about it . . .' She dropped her voice so Copernicus couldn't hear. 'The rats had to make a raft for themselves when they went over the dam. When Alfie blasted them away with water jets, they couldn't do anything about it. And cats – normal cats – hate water, don't they? It's all because the nine-lives bubble doesn't work in water! Cats know they can't be protected when they're wet; they know they could die!'

G-Mamma sucked her teeth, then raised an eyebrow. 'Impressive, Blonde. If you think you're right, prove it!'

Trouble was racing towards Janey, frantically trying to escape the snapping, five-headed beast snarling at his tail. 'Trubs, come here!' she called, patting her chest so that he leaped up into her arms. 'Now everybody grab a bucket!'

Jane Blonde held her Spycat in front of her and knelt on the floor. The rat-beast bounded towards them, baying for revenge. Janey didn't budge. The creature lunged, and Janey and Trouble were suddenly confronted with the creature's underbelly and the five gnashing hellhound heads.

'Claws out, Spycat!' she screamed.

Trouble instantly reached out his paw, flipped the sabre-edged claw out in front of him like a flick knife and allowed Janey to draw it along the water rats' shimmering skin shield, slicing through the gore like butter.

'Perfect!'

As the beast's front legs drew level with her head, Janey grabbed the power-hose and thrust it through the hole she had just made in the protective bubble. The creature sailed over her head as if impaled upon the hose, and Janey squeezed the trigger and let loose with the water. At full pressure it rocketed from the nozzle, driving a deluge between each of the rats. The five creatures shot in different directions across the forecourt, whipping around and spinning in the torrents.

'Now!' yelled Janey. Her father, G-Mamma, Alfie, Mrs Halliday and her mother leaped forward, each carrying a heavy metal bucket that they slammed down over the nearest rat. With a spy sitting on each bucket, and a steady supply of water to hand, there was no way they were going to get away this time. Copernicus and Paulette were snarling and squirming madly, and the Sun King mask had slipped a little to reveal the blackened maw that was his damaged throat.

Janey looked up, panting with relief, to congratulate the others, but stopped when she heard a smattering of applause from behind her. 'More!' somebody yelled. 'Best launch I've ever been to!' cried another voice.

The customers who'd been queuing to get the best deal at Abe 'n' Jean's Clean Machines lined the entrance to the car wash, whooping and clapping with all their might.

'They think we staged the whole thing!' said Jean Brown.

There was a long pause, and then someone said gently, 'We did.'

Abe Rownigan winked at Janey as he put his arm around Jean's shoulders. 'I'm sorry, Jean. In hindsight it was probably all a bit too realistic. But I'm glad we put on a good show. I mean, even you believed it.'

'I . . . Yes, I . . .' Janey's mother shook her head several times. 'What is this? What's going on?'

But there was no answer and the crowd was baying for more action. So after a few moments Jean Brown stepped up to the ribbon across the driveway to the car wash and karate-chopped it in half. She grinned at the clapping audience. 'Um, I . . . I declare Abe 'n' Jean's Clean Machines – open!'

'Don't you ever do that to me again, Abe Rownigan,' said Janey's mother as the customers drove in. She looked down at the metallic sheen of her bronze SPIsuit in bewilderment. 'Disappearing like that, and then all this. Never again. Do you promise?'

Janey looked on, a little tearfully, as Abe Rownigan took a ring from a little black box in his pocket. He put it on Jean's finger, then pressed her hand gently. 'I do, Jean Brown. I do.'

And he smiled regretfully as Janey's brain-wiped mother collapsed into her husband's arms.

furry ends

'So, let's get this straight,' said Alfie, hauling his bag up on his shoulder. 'Your Uncle Solomon, who we know is really your dad, Boz Brown, worked out this freezing thing and turned a frog into a mouse.'

'That's about it,' said Janey.

Alfie was still puzzled. 'Then he turned the Sun King's – well, Copernicus's – top spies into rats because they'd discovered the secret to a cat's nine lives? And ever since, my f— oh, I can't even say it – HE has been on a mission to get them changed back?'

'Yup.'

Janey hoped he would leave it at that – because there was something else she had to keep secret. The evenings that followed the car-wash incident had included some terribly serious conversations with her father and G-Mamma. Janey was adamant that nobody else – not even Alfie – was going to learn that her dad had actually used the Crystal Clarification Process to change one human into another. And she certainly wasn't going to tell them that he had performed the procedure on *himself* and was now living among them – as Abe! Only G-Mamma knew the truth.

'What about Paulette?' she asked, throwing Alfie off track. 'Are you interested in getting to know her more?'

'No way. Nor our f— HIM. How did Mum ever love somebody like that? She says he changed, but really, *that* much? Anyway, it's a bit difficult to get to know someone when they're a snowman. Or, you know. A snowgirl.'

'Yeah, I see what you mean.'

Everyone in the SPI unit had agreed that changing evil villains into living creatures was far too dangerous, so now a row of seven glistening statues lay preserved forever in a special freezer in a secret location far away.

Janey grinned at her friend. 'Now that's all sorted out, there is just one thing I'd like to know – that room behind the mops in the caretaker's cupboard? When we questioned Paulette she said she was in the cupboard because she had to get a message to her dad without anyone hearing. I honestly don't think she even knew about the secret room. So what's it all about?'

Alfie shrugged. 'Mum refused to tell me,' he said, looking at his watch. 'We're really early. Why don't we go and see for ourselves?'

The Spylets flitted through the half-empty corridors. From outside the caretaker's cupboard they could hear that the radio was playing to itself again and a deep male voice was humming along.

'Ready?' said Alfie. 'Now!'

They turned the handle and opened the door

together. The caretaker, complete with yellow rubber gloves, spun round from his bucket collection.

'Mr Saunders!' cried Janey.

Mr Saunders hastily removed the rubber gloves. 'Ah . . . hello. Um, oh dear . . . Look, I'd be grateful if you didn't tell anybody else about this, Janey, Alfie. I just . . . I just needed the extra money. And then your mother said I could use this funny little room behind the wall, and . . .'

'What for, sir?' asked Alfie.

Their teacher blushed furiously. 'For my band to practise in. The acoustics are really good in there, and I've soundproofed it with egg boxes . . .'

Janey suppressed a giggle. 'Don't worry, we won't tell anyone, Mr Saunders.' She couldn't imagine who would believe them anyway. A new song had just started on the radio. 'Er, Mr Saunders, do you know this song?'

It was the same one Abe Rownigan had recorded on her iPod.

Mr Saunders nodded. 'It's "Isn't She Lovely" by Stevie Wonder. He wrote it for his daughter when she was just born, I believe.'

And Janey smiled the biggest and widest grin ever.

When the Clean Jean van pulled up to the school gates that afternoon Jean Brown popped her head out of the window. 'You can get in next to me today, Janey.'

'What about Abe? Is he busy?' Janey threw her bag into a bucket and settled into the car. For two weeks she'd been banished to the back seat as Abe Rownigan supervised the early stages of the business launch, froze a few spies in his spare time and proved a dab hand at spaghetti bolognaise. Alfie declared his cooking to be even better than Clod's.

'Yes, but, um, not exactly,' said her mother, biting her lip. Suddenly she swerved into a parking space and turned to Janey. 'Abe won't be around much any more, Janey. He's gone up north today.'

Janey felt as though her heart had fallen through the floor of the car. 'He's gone? He can't have! Why?'

'He's got some other business interests he wants to pursue. We're so well set up already that Abe can just be a silent partner, and I can manage everything on my own.'

'What about you and him . . . what about him being my new father?' Tears spilled down Janey's cheeks.

'Oh, Janey. I know you liked him. And I did too. I still do! But we both just felt that we had too many other things going on. And just knowing him has made me stronger, Janey. It really has. I'm very happy with the business, and I'm very happy just being with you. But one day perhaps, because of Abe Rownigan, we'll both be ready to accept someone new.'

Janey slumped in her chair. 'What was so important he had to run off like that?'

'I don't know, some crisis with his next venture,' said Jean. 'Anyway, as I said, the new business doesn't sound my cup of tea at all. Something to do with . . . with metal underwear.'

196

There was an abrupt silence. 'Metal underwear?' said Janey. 'Do you mean . . . Copper Knickers?'

'That's it! Very odd idea. It must be a trade name for something.'

But Copernicus was safely incarcerated in a deep freeze. Janey sighed. It was her dad's message to her. He had tried to come back as a normal person, and it hadn't worked. It had put Janey and her mother in mortal danger. Now he'd gone away again for their sakes. Maybe they could never be together, just a normal family. That was the trade they had to make – the pay-off for being spies.

Her mum was watching her fearfully. Leaning over, Janey kissed her on the cheek. 'Come on, Mum. Fish and chips for tea.' Her dad's favourite.

'Chip shop here we come,' said Jean Brown.

After eating, Janey slipped through the fireplace to the Spylab. G-Mamma looked up guiltily. 'Caught me in the act! I just always wondered what Trouble would look like with curls.'

Trouble, who had been put through the Wower, mewed at Janey helplessly. A large ringlet drooped down over one of his huge green eyes. 'You OK, Trubs?' said Janey.

'Are *you* OK, Blonde-girl?' G-Mamma teased another roller out of his quiff.

Janey shrugged. 'Well, sort of. But my dad's disappeared. Again.'

'I thought as much when I saw he'd sent you a message.' Janey's SPI:KE swivelled around on her stool and clicked open an email. 'Can't tell iggly squiggly of what he's on about, as usual.'

Janey looked hard at the email entitled 'Sorry, sweetheart, but'. There were just four words:

furri ends
no oS

'It's the rats, isn't it? Furry ends.' said G-Mamma.

Janey played with the letters in her mind – and soon knew what the message really said.

f(ur)riends
nooS

She grinned. 'It's all about you, G-Mamma. You, and the others.'

'I do NOT have a furry end! I can't speak for your mother, of course, but—'

'No,' soothed Janey. 'It's kind of a dingbat. It's a nice message. He says, "*Sorry sweetheart, but you are surrounded by friends. Back soon.*"'

'Oh!' G-Mamma whirled around on her chair with a smug smile on her round face. 'That's all right then, Blonde!'

Janey Brown was a fully trained Spylet. And next time evil came knocking, Jane Blonde would be ready.

She nodded contentedly. 'Yes, G-Mamma. It is.'